I0534824

DOOM NIGHT
Death of Civilization

JOHN E. ELIN

BAYSCOUT PUBLISHING

Doom Night
Death of Civilization

John E. Elin

Paperback Edition ISBN-10: 0-9975390-0-3
Paperback Edition ISBN-13: 978-0-9975390-0-4
Kindle Edition ISBN -10: 0-9975390-1-1
Kindle Edition ISBN -13: 978-0-9975390-1-1

Published by Bayscout Publishing

Printed in USA

DOOM NIGHT

DEDICATION

To my wife who is the best person I have ever known.

CONTENTS

ACKNOWLEDGMENTS

Thanks to the teachers, editors, friends, coworkers, and family for their support, comments, critique, and interest. Their encouragement has given me the courage and energy to finish this book.

PART I FRIENDLIES

CHAPTER ONE

My name is Brock. I lived in a small rural Midwestern town. We passed time watching TV, playing video games, and hunting. Everyone considered me tall for a twelve-year-old. We were not a wealthy family. My maternal grandparents lived on a farm with many animals. I spent summers on their farm working and playing. There is an ugly scar on my arm. I had an accidental run in with a pitchfork in the hayloft. In school, I played on the baseball team as a first baseman with friends. Baseball was the most important sport in our town.

I found myself lost in muddy fields stretching as far as I could see. I recall being at home with my mother when it happened. She was reading the newspaper as she did every night before bedtime. I was on the floor watching a sci-fi movie.

An overwhelming deafening boom shook the entire house. Everything was vibrating and made noise. It sounded like our wooden boards on the floor were lifting from the nails. I felt a hot blast of electrified air. I saw splinters of glass from shattered windows and wood flying through the room. A large piece of glass from our picture window hit my mother in the head. Then everything went dark.

The flying debris in my house knocked me out. I awoke confused, thirsty, hungry, outside, and lost. Nothing in sight was taller than the small bushes behind humps of burned ground. The air was hot and filled with swirling dust. The heated air had scorched my clothes off, and I lay there partially naked, scared, and shivering from shock. My hands and body were red from heat and my throat burned. The burned hair on my head felt short and hard. I tried to stand, but my hands hurt too much to support me. I rolled over and belly-crawled. The rough ground scratched my bare stomach. I tried to keep going until I didn't have enough energy to continue. The pain made me want to sleep. I fell asleep, not knowing what to expect when I awoke.

I must have slept for hours and would've gone on longer but the splatter of big warm raindrops interrupted my sleep. The sky was a hazy yellow from rusty brown rain. The discolored rainfall had changed the ground color. My skin turned a shade of reddish brown. The big raindrops stung my scorched body. I had to find shelter. A small bush ahead might provide protection.

Lying on my belly, I used my palms and tips of my toes to shuffle forward. It seemed like an eternity, but finally the mound was within reach with a few more scoots, I would be near the top.

When I reached the top, I couldn't slip under the low hanging bush. I propped myself up, raised my head, and stretched out to see the surrounding area. I swung my head back and forth peering through the rain to spot something: a building, a car, rubbish, anything. A large flat board floated in a puddle. I rolled over the mound and slid down the incline to the puddle's edge. I reached out for the board and pulled it over to cover my body. The board pressed down on my sore body. I heard rain driving hard against it. It was soaking wet and heavy but sheltered me from the rain. As it laid on my face, I felt my breath bouncing back, making me feel alive.

Down deep inside, I felt lost and very scared. I remember murmuring repeatedly, "Mom, Mom." Then I fell asleep but not for long. The lack of splattering sounds woke me. It took a few seconds to remember the nightmare I had escaped earlier and a few more to believe it was still happening. I pushed the board off me. The sky was brighter. I guessed it was daytime. Lying flat out on a small slope, I felt the unexplained burns. The dried dirty rain had painted me brown. Besides that, I could hear my stomach growling for food.

The nap had helped to ward off the shock. Slowly, I moved my knee under me then used my hands to push myself upright. I wiped the crust off my face and peered over the land. My eyes barely opened because of the sticky junk in the rain.

It looked as if someone had taken a gigantic ice scraper and smeared it across the ground. Nothing in sight was recognizable. Worst of all, I didn't see another person in any direction. No people with brown muddy lumps scattered here, there, and everywhere. Where was I? This couldn't be my neighborhood without houses, trees, streets, or cars.

Thrown to the ground, and left for dead in the desolate landscape made me feel like something dragged me into another world without food, water, and shelter.

I scanned the horizon. Once I thought I saw something sticking up, above mounds of dirt. I kept looking in that direction until my eyes played games on me. The ground appeared to jump around, so I determined it was nothing but my jumbled-up brain playing tricks on me. The air appeared to be clearing because I could see farther and farther. Sick and shaking from fright, I saw nothing in any direction.

Straight ahead, a wisp of wind opened a gap in the dirty air. I glimpsed something rigid and upright, but then the gap closed. Standing up, I walked straight towards it without thinking. I hoped it wouldn't be far. I was going crazy.

With every step, my feeling of hopelessness grew. The hunger and fatigue beat my spirits lower. I plowed through mud pushing myself while daydreaming about getting there and finding other people to help me. There would be tons of hot food with comforting warmth.

Ahead, a large object was sticking up. I rushed towards it, falling clumsily, and then forcing myself back up to my feet.

It was the hood of a car. Mud covered the engine so I couldn't see it. Tilted up on one side, it had no passengers or driver alive or dead.

I was happy to see the intact car. It would make a great place to keep me warm and dry. I looked for something to pry the side window open. There was a large stick behind the car. I tried to open the window with it, but it was too big. Kicking the window with my shoe-less muddy feet did nothing but leave muddy tracks. I had to find something heavy like a rock or cement block. Searching on my hands and knees, I groped for a hard protrusion. Halfway around the car, I found a hard surface. After digging into soft mud, I found a piece of broken concrete. It looked like part of a sidewalk. I dug around it to get it in my hands. I pulled and pulled, but nothing broke loose. A wire was attached. I kept digging to get the first section of concrete exposed enough where I could swing it back and forth. It finally broke loose. I took it, went to the car window, and banged on it until the glass splintered into small jagged squares. After peeling it away, I climbed into the car, then into the backseat, where I collapsed.

CHAPTER TWO

My world had become scary and dangerous. Someone or something could sneak up on me and hurt me, so I considered just staying put but I couldn't quit. Although having a place to hide out, sleep, and keep dry made me feel better, it didn't take care of my hunger. I was accustomed to stuffing my mouth with drink or food every few hours. I wondered how long I was out. It didn't matter. I was starving and felt thin as a noodle. Lack of water and the heat made my tongue swollen and dry.

The glove box had a pack of matches and an old screwdriver. A screwdriver might work as a tool or a weapon. The matches would be safe, dry, and easy to find in the glove box. I looked up above the front windshield and spotted the car mirror. I climbed into the front seat and looked at my reflection. It was difficult to see with the dim light from outside. I hardly recognized my own face because it was so gaunt, pale, and dirty with dark eyes.

My growling stomach, reminded me to search for food and water. I slid myself feet first through the window, lifted my butt up and over while avoiding a small puddle of water. I stood up by the open hood trying to figure out which way to head without losing my way back. If I headed out into acres of field with no houses or businesses, I could walk for miles with no hope of finding any landmarks.

The brown goop covered the mushy ground, looking back, my footsteps, were noticeable. In the far distance, a roof was sticking out just above ground. In the other direction, fallen trees had stacked up against a rock. The trees looked like logs stripped of their leaves and branches. Nothing was moving in any direction. I found no sign of life.

I proceeded to the rooftop. Stepping carefully, I avoided spots with water buildup because they could be deep holes. My footsteps were still visible.

Traveling up and down mounds of dirty wet muddy dunes was tedious. At each step, I tested for support and dug in my toes so as not to slip. The roof looked bigger and bigger with each step. It belonged to a small building. After reaching it, I was afraid to climb on top. What if it couldn't support me? There was nothing to see under it. On one side, a small window with the glass broken out was sticking up above the mud. Moving closer to the building, I knelt down and peeked in. It was a small smelly restroom. I could see a toilet and urinal. Both looked dirty as if someone had taken rusty rainwater and sprayed it into the room. I could barely see the exit that stood closed. Not giving it much thought, I put my legs through the window and set my feet on the toilet back. I stepped down into mud slurry on the floor. The stink of feces filled the air. Moving towards the door, I hoped for the best. There was no pitter patter of small claws, panting, or squeaking sounds from animals.

I turned the door handle. As it opened, pressure shoved me back against the wall. In came a stream of mud covering me up to my ankles. A fallen wall was halfway blocking the exit.

Pulling myself over the wall allowed me to move into the next room. There was no mud there. I stood leaning over to avoid hitting my head on the low hanging ceiling. Scary creaking noises from every direction frightened me. It had to be settling, which meant this wreck of a building could be dangerous. Slowly groping around in the dark, I ran into what felt like a store counter. Underneath, I felt smooth tile. A food odor replaced the awful restroom smell.

My eyes hadn't adjusted to the absolute darkness. I was scurrying through the dark, sniffing out my next meal. I swept my hands across the floor and felt something soft and wrapped in paper. Being curious, I grabbed it then climbed back up to the counter top. It was a pack of M & M's. I ripped open the package and placed a couple in my mouth. The sugar made my mouth water. I had to have more.

Laying all fears aside, I hung my legs over the counter and slipped to the floor. It gave way and moved down as if it was part of a seesaw. I fell on my butt landing with a thud. The short free fall caused me to feel fear swell up in my groin. More M & M's slid down from the seesaw high side hitting my thighs. I reached out for the closest package. Right then, I was too hungry to worry about the unsteady floor. Those M & M's went down so fast it caused me to choke. I laid there feeling the fullness and the energy from the banquet.

It was dead quiet. I heard myself breathing. Remembering my predicament brought me back to my senses. I must find more food.

Having faced tough challenges in the last few hours, I had to keep going. I couldn't be content with having found a few M & M's and expect someone or something to come along and save me. I could end up starving to death. The idea frightened me. I had to stay tough and focused to survive.

Like in war movies, where a hero would jump up and blast away at the enemy. They most always survived the beatings and deprivation. They always escaped back to their own lines by lying low and making the best of the weather and meager rations. I pictured myself as one of those heroes.

I stood up on the wobbly tilted floor with my toes pointed upward. I slid backwards on the angled floor. My butt ran into something cold and hard that forced me to change directions. I paused long enough to collect the M & M's. I gathered up ten packages and threw them onto the counter.

After a few shuffles forward, the floor seesawed downward. Once the floor tilted down to the bottom, I attempted to stand. That was a mistake. I should have put my hands above my head. The incline had made me tilt down towards the floor and when I straightened up all the way, bang! I felt the burn from a cut on my temple as blood ran down my face. I cautiously reached up towards what cut me. A big wooden beam with sharp splinters stuck out from the wall. The cut seemed to be small, but bleeding a lot. I felt drops running down from my chin. I repeated over and over in my head, take it slow, and be careful.

This stupid mistake couldn't stop me. I had to find the stored food. Back down on my hands and knees, I moved forward with one hand out in front, reached a wall, and followed it as it turned in a different direction. My hand brushed something soft. I pulled at it. It felt like a towel or a cover with straps. It was an apron. As I crawled farther along the floor, I tried not to catch the long apron under my knees.

My hands felt something in front that recoiled when I touched it. I pulled my hand back. The place was getting spooky. It was a small can. Happily, the M & M's had already taken care of my immediate hunger or I would have been tearing at the tin. There were two more. I made the apron into a bag, placed the cans into it, and dragged it with one fist, using my other hand as a feeler. I found the wall again and followed along it. Against the wall, a stove stood with a large dirty greasy flat top. Continuing while reaching out with my free hand, I felt a sticky, smelly, gooey mess of something in front of me. It was a rancid gravy or old thick soup. It made me consider turning back.

I'd never spent so much time in a dark risky place. My eyes saw things moving that were unreal. It was like when you close your eyes tight and see things jumping or flying. Exploring in the darkness was making me uneasy and panicky. What I was facing was harder to overcome because of my imagination kept playing games in my head.

I was thankful I had found candy, eaten, and discovered the cans. I needed to return to the car with the goodies.

Back at the seesaw floor, the jagged piece of wood caused no problem. I crossed over the counter, moved towards the collapsed wall and restroom, then climbed into the smelly, muddy, and dimly lit restroom. Stepping up on the toilet, I swung the apron through the open window, then grabbed the metal sill and pulled myself up through the window. It was great to be free from the dark dusty dungeon. I had moved slowly and carefully.

My footprints were easy to find. There was no hint of anything above ground that might lead me to more supplies. As I walked "home," I became curious to see what was in the cans. Stopping to look, I found cans of beans, mushrooms, olives, and a can of sardines. After all that scrounging around, I ended up with two cans of chewy bits and a can of stinky fish. At least, the beans would supply much needed protein. It was a very lucky find.

I wanted to catch sight of someone else. The quiet loneliness made me feel worried and fearful no matter how manly I was determined to be. I had too many questions about it all and I needed to find answers to feel secure.

Mud covered my body, scalp scalded bald and dry blood on my cheek trailing down to my chest. What

9

would another human think of me? They'd probably run away thinking I was a dangerous nut.

I folded the apron back into its pouch shape and continued the trek back up and down the mounds following my footprints. I imagined my tracks headed off to an unknown place that still had clean air, clean water, and delicious food.

When I reached the car, I tossed the apron in then climbed through the window. Luckily, I was slender for a twelve-year-old, else, all this climbing into small windows would have been much more difficult. I hopped into the backseat and put the food on the floor. I took the apron, covered myself, lay back across the seat, and closed my eyes.

The images of the day pranced through my mind, hot rain, the board, the car hood, the rooftop, and finally crawling in the dark in search of food. It had taken all my courage to pass through the absolute blackness inside the building's guts.

The stash of food below my feet and cozy backseat lessened my worry. My body was tingling with healing and as I dozed off, I felt strangely different. I dreamed about my dad and how I hadn't seen him for such a long time. I slept deeply while dreaming about family picnics. We played lots of baseball and volleyball. The adults always gave us extra strikes and never put us out as we ran bases. I pictured green grass in parks with flowered blankets spread around packages of food and baskets of goodies. I remembered dipping into the old washtub for ice cubes and sipping on sugary tea. Best of all, the taste of homemade ice cream came to mind. I remembered how we used big spoons to scoop it up into our mouths until our mothers would see us and shoo us away. I felt happiness from those times in my dreams. While sleeping, I was oblivious to the perils of this existence because there my mother was alive and life was wonderful even though I hadn't known how wonderful.

CHAPTER THREE

This nap seemed longer than the others. When I awoke, I felt unusual. I felt I had more than before, yet I was unaware of what it might be. I remembered the M & M's and ate some. The beans, mushrooms, olives, and fish were not appealing. Not yet, anyway. The M & M's and small stinky fish couldn't last long.

I had to return to the crushed building for more food. I jumped into the front seat and reached back for the apron. I slid through the passenger window, stood up, and hung the apron around my neck. It was too long and wide for me, so I appeared to be wearing a dress.

The tracks to the crushed building were visible. Since my booty of food was not a big burden, I took it too. I wasn't ready to leave such valuable resources abandoned. Who knows what might happen, in this newly created wilderness. I gathered up the food from the car and wrapped it in the apron. I hooked the loop around my shoulder so it was a lot like carrying a shoulder bag.

Turning towards the twice-traveled trail, I marched away. The trip seemed shorter. I guess it was because I knew what to expect. When I arrived at the roof again, I stooped down by the window and listened for critters like rats, cats, and dogs. Nothing sounded an alarm.

I dropped the apron down into the window. I slipped down and felt around for my apron. I didn't want to drag food back into the dark hole so I took it out and piled it in the sink right next to the toilet. My confidence was high. If I had a flashlight, I could have rushed right in while avoiding holes and sharp objects. My bulging eyeballs strained to capture images that only my imagination supplied. The counter was easy to find. I made sure I stayed with the crawling. The crawling kept me lower and spread my weight out. I couldn't risk the standing crouched position because more jagged edges were possible. I reached the gooey mess and realized I had to head deeper into the uncharted zone.

Along the wall with the messy floor, I found pots and pans. It was strange to hear them bang together as I moved forward. I felt a sense of urgency. It could have been the increase in creaking noises. They were enough to make me worried. Crawling deeper into the abyss of darkness was not helping.

Reaching the back wall without finding anymore provisions wasn't a good sign. Following the wall around, I ran into more aprons and towels on the floor. A linen closet had exploded onto the floor. I grabbed a couple more aprons, three towels and shoved them into my makeshift pouch.

Just when I was thinking about the way back and how my knees were hurting, I hit a jackpot. As I swung my hands, I felt cans. Oh goody, more stinky fish. I took the two aprons and made them into bags. This made three bags for food collection. I waded right into the cans. It didn't take long to fill the first apron.

After filling the second and third aprons, I had to rest. I laid my head down on one apron, took a deep breath, and closed my eyes. A few minutes later, I heard loud creaking sounds. I realized this building was unsafe. I snatched up the aprons. A much louder bang, sounding like a snapped tree limb caused the air to vibrate from the noise while filling the room with choking dust. My eyes teared up and my tongue tasted chalky from the powdery dust.

I went into full skedaddle mode. I tugged on all three heavy aprons at the same time. They were too bulky and heavy. I split them apart and put them on my shoulders, then rose onto my feet in a squatting position. The bulkiest apron slipped over my right shoulder. The others hung over my left shoulder. For balance, I moved one straight in front of me. I held my hands in front of me feeling for the wall and any obstacles.

The noises were coming from the last wall I had found. I hurried to the collapsed wall but not without going back down on my knees to pass under the low ceiling. In a few minutes, I would climb back into the restroom. The heavy aprons and awkward duck walking caused me to fall a couple times. I was racing with the creaking and collapsing building. Around the corner, I went with my butt almost dragging on the ground. I felt safer having reached the seesaw floor. I heard a slow crashing sound that lasted forever. The seesaw floor wobbled under my feet.

One apron slipped loose, and I heard cans hitting the floor. Thankfully, others stayed in the bag. I clung to the last two full aprons. I had to keep them or all this work and danger would have been for nothing. Regaining use of my feet, I stayed low trying not to panic.

After scooting over to the seesaw end, I pushed the aprons on to the counter top, being careful not to lose another can. After a loud rumbling noise, the counter heaved up and knocked me to the floor just as I raised my leg to cross over it.

Bricks tumbled down on my legs. I covered my head with my hands just before they hit it. By the time they stopped, they had covered my legs and made them almost numb. Using my best hand, I reached down and pushed the bricks off my legs. They hurt, especially where the bricks had torn into my shins. I sat against the wall for a minute trying to feel them. I kneeled, grabbed the counter, and slipped over to the floor. My precious aprons had made it. Dragging the aprons on the floor, I limped to the collapsed wall by the restroom.

I swung the aprons over the wall into the restroom, climbed over the wall and slipped into the stinky muddy restroom. Standing on the toilet, I pushed two full aprons through the window. I opened the partially filled apron, threw my food from the sink into it, and passed it through the window.

Slipping my head out and with one hard thrust, I escaped. I grabbed the aprons, stood up, and limped away from the building. When I was far away, I sat on the ground to rest. My legs and hands were sore from the bricks. My body was throbbing from the hard work and pain.

As I was taking notice of my scratches, bruises, welts, and sore areas, I heard more loud crashing sounds accompanied by ground shaking. A plume of dust whooshed up where my window entrance had been. The ground sunk down around the roof. It cracked, as if it was a piece of pottery. I had survived a life threatening ordeal for my three homemade pouches of food and it was worth it. The experience had exhausted and weakened me. The temperature was turning cold. I reached down into the aprons and pulled out the towels. I took one apron and placed it up as a pillow. The towels made great covers. I fell asleep on the ground, knowing my booty was safe.

CHAPTER FOUR

When I awoke, I knew another day had passed. I was groggy and maybe in shock from the narrow escape. I felt an itchy tickling from the cut on my head. As I touched my head, I saw a blur of motion. There were insects like gnats feeding on my blood. I brushed them away, stood up, and took a quick glance up and down my body for signs of other bugs. These were the first living things I'd seen since this started. They were small living things, but if I was still alive and these pesky bugs were flying around, then maybe others had survived and my daydreams would come true. The bugs were like messengers telling me to keep hoping.

I didn't want to accept that I was by myself. I kept thinking at any second my mother would appear from behind the hills surrounding me. She'd be calling out, "Brock, Brock." I would run to her arms for a hug.

I reached out for an apron and opened it wide. There in front of me was a dream come true, a bottle of spring water. There were four sports type bottles with the nozzle on the cap. I found more bottles of soda and it felt like Christmas. Finally, I had something to drink. I got the bottle of water and gulped it vigorously. While being tempted by the other bottles in my pouches, I remembered my earlier mantra, "Take it slow, and be careful." I picked up the aprons and began the trip back to the car.

My homemade bags were on my skinny shoulders and my tracks were easy to see and follow. I was happy the gnats weren't gnawing at my face or flocking around me in their pestering ways. When I arrived at the car, I walked around it, checking for tracks or anything that looked out of place. Everything was fine, so I crawled into the window. After jumping into the backseat, I grabbed a pack of M & M's, ripped it open, and go them up.

To count the cans, I stacked them on the floorboard. The count was better than expected. I had seventeen new cans. There were three cans of beef stew, three cans of corned-beef hash, four cans of carrots, four cans of spinach, and three cans of baby peas. The water in the cans would supplement the bottles of water and soda. The food in the cans was edible as-is.

It was early in the day. My choice was to rest or leave on another scouting trip. I still needed more supplies and perhaps a sturdier shelter. The choice was clear.

It occurred to me that I needed a better way to mark my trail. The wind or rain could erase my tracks. I remembered how Hansel and Gretel left crumbs for trail markers. If they hadn't been edible, their plan would've worked. I used the screwdriver and stabbed the seat cover until I could pull out stuffing. I stashed the stuffing into my apron. Maybe this was overkill, but I didn't have a keen sense of direction.

I faced a big decision. Which way to go? The roof in the distance was gone. Turning full circle, I couldn't see any other object. Arbitrarily, I walked the opposite direction of collapsed roof.

Off I trotted, counting my steps to keep track of how far I'd gone. I would push markers into the ground or gather up pebbles or dirt clods to hold them in place every three hundred steps. While putting down the second marker, I discovered a big stick almost the size of a broomstick, but shorter and thicker. Without a second thought, I picked it up and used it as a staff. It kept me balanced while supporting me. When the mounds were closer together, I used it to pole vault over the small dips. This made traveling less boring and definitely faster. I counted each leap as one step. I used my fingers holding the bag to register thousands so I wouldn't have to keep counting using thousand repeatedly.

Nothing around me hinted that civilization existed. Not yet. When I made it to two thousand, my middle finger became the second thousand. Three thousand five hundred steps seemed like a bunch of steps, but it was most likely less than a half-mile. My strips for trail marking were holding out well. If the terrain had been flatter, the car hood would be visible behind me. It was getting hilly. At the top of hills, I stopped and spun around looking for signs of civilization.

Six thousand steps in one direction and finally I saw something ahead. Could it be another car or smashed building? As I approached, I determined it was a corner of a block wall. It turned out to be a building, yet beyond, flies were swirling around in a large dark cloud. From a distance, they had blended in with the wall. I wondered what made them hover there. I remembered how they had made themselves at home on my sores. As I went over the last mound, two bodies lay in front of me, a large man, and a kid my size. The bugs fully covered them so they appeared to have black crawly skin. They were nearly nude. I guessed whatever burned my shirt and hair away, got them too and if that didn't strip them, the mudflow would've finished the job. They were definitely goners.

Until then, I hadn't ever seen a dead person except in pictures or on television programs. The scene that lay before me seemed unreal. I wasn't ready to face it so I turned around and darted back to my path and counting.

Finally, at nine thousand three hundred steps, I

recognized something hopeful. A two-story house had floated on the mud. It looked odd sunken in on one corner with nothing around it. Like me, the dirty rain had recolored it. All the windows were without glass. Seeing something of this size above ground was a good sign. I approached towards the front porch where the mailbox was still hanging. On the outside, the house was a wreck. Siding had fallen off, leaving black tar paper exposed. The screen door was hanging by a hinge. Pausing outside for a minute before deciding to rummage around inside, the narrow escape from the collapsed building came to mind.

I set my staff on the ground, put on my apron, and entered the front door. The first room had a chair rail with wainscoting. I saw an armchair in the lowest corner. Other than that, it was empty. In the next room I found a cracked up china cabinet with one broken cup. Next was the kitchen. An empty side-by-side refrigerator lay on the floor with one door busted. I was hoping it would have food. I looked in the cupboards. Not one morsel of food anywhere.

I returned to the first room and found a stairwell. The stairs had collapsed into the basement. The slender passage to the upstairs was in place. Putting my right hand on one wall and the left stretched to the other, I pushed out. Using my feet in the same way, I could shimmy up the wall to the top. I had done this many times before at my grandmother's store between two buildings set apart about the same distance as the stairwell. I had named this technique the invisible stairs. It took seven invisible steps to reach the top. At the top, I gave one last push while swinging my knee up to hook the floor. It was enough.

I found one door hanging on hinges. The other rooms were door-less. My eyes caught sight of something that looked promising in the room on the left. I moved towards the room on the angled and weakened buckled up hardwood floor. This was the second floor. I could easily fall through it.

I found shirts, pants, and underwear. All were for adults. The filthy rain had gotten through the broken windows enough to make all of them stained. I took all I could carry. I scooted around the room filling up my arms and hanging them on my shoulders. Returning to the stairwell, I tossed them downstairs past the hole. In the next room, I found more clothes and loose jewelry. Some clothes were for a woman. The jewelry was a tangled mess of necklaces and beaded bracelets. I took the jewelry, too. I threw it and the last armful of clothes down the stairwell and moved on to the next room.

In one corner, I found toys, including a metal piggy bank. The bank resembled a tractor. I jiggled the bank and heard coins rattling. I grabbed it up for the trip back. The only room left was a bathroom with the toilet still attached. A cracked bathtub and a sink held up by pipes hung loose from the wall. I pushed the sink, and it swung back and forth. A small towel closet was wide open. I climbed the shelves and looked inside the top ones. A package of white toilet paper with four rolls was on the top shelf. Splintered wood caught the rolls. I tugged on it. It came out easily. I felt the paper. It was clean and soft. It felt strange to find something not rough, hard, or dirty. I tore off a piece of paper, spit on it, and wiped off my face. I looked at the stool and toilet paper and felt an urge to go to the bathroom. When I finished, I closed the lid and left. The furniture and furniture parts were not of any use in my situation. Propped up high above the mud made the house inviting. I had followed my motto. I had taken it slow, and I had been careful.

Making it down the staircase was easy. I looked down at the clothes and picked out a large Levis shirt. I put it on and rolled up the sleeves. It hung down almost to my knees. I tugged at the twisted up jewelry, pulling one necklace out. I put it over my head and felt the smooth white oval beads. My red burned body was not feeling trapped in my new attire because it was so roomy. Picking up my stack of clothes, jewelry, piggy bank, and toilet paper, I started outside to follow my markers back to the car.

Something caught my eye near the armchair. It was small and shiny. My arms were full of bulky clothes. I dropped them. It was a small compact with the mirror still intact. My mother used one when we were out shopping.

I had given my face a spit bath with the toilet paper. In the compact mirror, my face looked much better than in the car mirror. It was as if I was recognizing myself again from before this mess started. I put the compact in my shirt pocket then returned to the pile of clothes. The piggy bank and jewelry would be safer on the apron bottom with clothes stuffed on top. The apron couldn't hold all the clothes.

I went outside, picked up my stick, found my markers, and headed back to my haven.

The humidity was high and breathing was tough in the misty stale air. I thought it was sweat on my forehead dripping into my eyes. The mist turned into a drizzle. Until then, I had no problem finding the markers. My tracks were clear. I didn't count steps. I left the markers in the ground as I passed them. The rain poured down harder. For a short while, I didn't care because it barely beat down my tracks and left the markers intact.

Then everything changed. I heard a roar behind me. Turning around, I could clearly see the house but the rain coming towards me was a gray wall of water. It resembled a giant wave coming from the sky. The drops caused a roar as they battered the ground. I remembered the rusty brown rain and how much of a struggle that was. I panicked and ran towards the next marker. The clothes were getting wet from the rain. Holding them pressed against my body was making me run with a waddle because I couldn't freely swing my arms. The apron on my back was swinging wildly. I felt my staff hitting my shins. I heard the coins rattling in the piggy bank. In a short time, the heavy rain caught up with me. I slipped down a slope and fell face forward. I gathered the clothes back up and included the jewelry and piggy bank. The torn toilet paper wrapper allowed the paper to become soaked. The four rolls of fluff had turned into wet heavy rocks. No matter, I wouldn't give up on them. I kept them in the package.

Breathing heavily from the effort, made me feel faint. I was running on the mud and stumbled often. I jumped over a large hard-to-see hole then looked straight ahead. I froze. It wasn't what I saw, but what I did not see that shocked me. The rain had quickly passed through, yet it had done damage. Where the clear footprints had been before, nothing but smooth dirt remained. The next marker was no longer in sight.

Two days had passed. I had suppressed the knowledge that my family may be gone. The gruesome bodies covered with bugs hadn't upset me too much. However, turmoil and loneliness made me scream while tears streamed down my face. I dropped the clothes, jewelry, and paper. Down on my knees I fell, with both fists clenched while hammering the ground.

I cried out, "Why? Why?" Why did I have to suffer like this? What did I do to deserve this? I didn't even know to whom I was screaming. It was sadness, fear, torture, and confusion that may or may not have spelled doom. The rain had destroyed my well thought-out plan. I had to let it out. The hard demeanor wasn't the real me. The child left in me had to express itself. I felt sorry for myself, thinking I was only a small boy. I couldn't be blamed. Curled up in a fetal position feeling my warmth moved me into calm restful peace.

My stomach was growling again. I felt the emptiness that was right next to the pain in my heart. Do I want to keep going? The image of my mother and dad was vivid. It gave me a warm feeling to remember them when we were all still living together before their divorce. It was a way to avoid the truth about their breakup and not share any blame for it. My mom would get scared at night after he left. I told her I was there for her and if anyone came around, I would protect her. I pictured the glass flying.

It made me angry because whatever happened to them had made me feel helpless, afraid, and sad. I had managed not to let their arguments cause me not to love them. I wondered if any others in my family had survived and if something normal still existed.

My sobbing stopped. I remember saying aloud to myself, "You are a man." I had to continue. Self-preservation made quitting a non-choice.

CHAPTER FIVE

I couldn't afford to dwell on the past because satisfying my hunger and being safe took priority. I stood up and faced the direction I thought was right, knowing my panicked run could have gotten me off track. The first sign of change hit while closing my eyes to think. Not only did I see the markers right in front of me, but all others leading to the car. When I opened my eyes, I still saw nothing on the ground. The torrent of rain had washed away the footprints and the markers.

What was I seeing in my head? I closed them again and there before me was the ground as it appeared with my footprints. It was as if I'd made a mental imprint of them. All I had to do was shut my eyes to stay on track. Yet, it was more. It was an entire trail from the house to my car with recognizable hills and mounds. Was I asleep dreaming this? It couldn't be. I didn't know if I could trust what I was seeing. Maybe it was a mirage, only visible with my closed eyes. Maybe I'd gone crazy.

When I turned in a different direction, the vision did not stay right in front of me as if it was tracking to my movements. It was visible in the direction I should be following. What could I lose by following it? This was unnatural. I just kept going with my eyes open. After walking awhile, I closed my eyes to see if I'd strayed from the trail. It was still there. It was an instinct like the swallows knowing the way to Capistrano, or the salmon returning to lay eggs at the same spot where they were born. However, this was different because I saw the entire thing. Maybe they did too? Perhaps, this was how humans experienced the world before we created maps and road signs. Whatever had left this land barren and devastated made me different.

Making my way back to the car, I passed the wall where I found the two bodies and wondered if they were still swarming with bugs. I didn't intend to get close to that scene again. The ground was mushy from the rain making the trek tiresome. I was halfway back when I stopped to rest. Sitting on top of a mound, I looked for signs of life. There were no sounds or movement. I wondered if I would ever see another person. I remembered the food back at the car. The corned-beef hash would be something different from the M & M's. I felt happiness creeping back. I felt a smile on my face. This wasn't a place to count blessings, in the open, exposed to whatever dangers this new world would bring.

I found out how true that was. As I was daydreaming, there was a movement on my left side. It was flash of color different from the dull landscape around me. There were no worrisome sounds. Even so, the stubby hair left on my body stood straight up. My senses were on full alert. Danger was coming to visit. I picked up my staff and slipped down behind the mound, opposite the movement. I pulled the clothes and apron closer.

I heard scratching and sniffing sounds. I glanced at my staff and noted it was blunt at both ends. I heard a small yelping noise coming from in front of me. That's when it exposed itself. Crouching down close to the ground with its head kept low, I didn't recognize it. The large dog had the posture of a hunter ready to strike. I raised my staff to take a swing at it. Before I could swing, another dog jumped on my back. Its nails dug into me. Then its jaws snapped at my neck just missing getting a good grip. The dog in front had distracted me.

His loud growling sounded vicious and he meant to kill me. He had me on my stomach. I rolled over to face the next attempt to bite me, pushing my staff in front. The dog bit the stick. Its fangs were hanging over the top. Smelly saliva was drooling from its mouth. His bugged-out eyes looked cold and evil. I held on to the stick with one hand tugging at it to keep the beast hooked. I reached for my apron and swung it towards his head. The piggy bank hit solid on top of its head. The dog let loose of the stick and perhaps fell dead.

I remembered the other dog and rolled towards the opposite direction. When I looked up, I was staring right into its mouth. I still had the stick and apron but the dog had the advantage with the upper ground. I let the apron fall and grabbed the stick with both hands. The dog jumped into the air down towards me. I thrust the stick at its gut hoping to stop it in midair. Its stomach was stronger than I expected and yet the blow garnered a yelp while scaring the dog farther away.

It hadn't finished. The blow made it more ferocious. I grabbed the apron, stood up, and swung the heavy end at it. It dodged my swings while snapping at me, then its teeth sunk into my calf. The bite made me feel strange. I twisted around, reached down with both hands, and grabbed the dog's hind legs tightly. The extra pull where it had my leg caused a little added pain. I twisted the dog's legs so much that its spine twisted. That was enough for it to release its bite. Holding the legs tightly, I swung it around with my arms extended. Its head whirled out away from me. I was getting dizzy. The dog's weight increased my speed. I let go. It flew towards a mound of dirt. I heard it cry out as it crumpled to the ground.

This battle was finished. The first dog was dead or

knocked out. The second one realized taking me on had been a mistake. It got to all fours and glanced back at me. My eyes stared into his and my dominance was enough to make it bow its head and scurry away. I spun around as the other dog moved. A couple minutes had passed since I had beaten it. I took my staff and hit him hard on the head. I struck his back, too. If this thing lived, it would remember me from the beating I gave it.

I worried that I could catch rabies from the bloodied bite on my calf. I took a blouse from an apron and wrapped around my lower leg. Carrying the aprons, clothes, and staff, I closed my eyes, and the trail appeared. I veered away from the beaten dog just in case it had enough energy to jump at me. By then, my rage had subsided, and I didn't want to kill it. The bite tingled and caused me to limp more. Those dogs were smart. It was lucky only two of them showed. I had planned nothing, just reacted. I said to myself aloud, "Those dogs didn't know how tough I am. They had picked on the wrong victim." I promised myself if they returned; I would kill them both.

The dogs were a real wake up call. I remember recognizing that the bugs meant other things had survived. It never crossed my mind that something could be hunting humans.

I followed the trail and sometimes I saw a real piece of seat stuffing. When I saw the car hood, it meant my vision thing I had, worked. It also meant I could crawl into the backseat and cuddle up with all my new treasures.

Sliding into the backseat, I opened the apron and put the bank on the floor. My staff was on the front seat leaning toward the backseat. I put it there in case I had to grab it. I had to play this game to survive. There were mean things outside that would rather eat me than look at me. I dug around in the cans until I found corned-beef hash. I used the screwdriver to poke holes in the top and to enlarge the holes. The top opened wide enough to let me get clumps out with my fingers. I stuck the screwdriver in it to stir it. Its aroma filled the air.

The first bite tasted salty, a real contrast to M & M's. It was so good. I grabbed a bottle of soda and used the screwdriver to push the cap off. It was warm delicious soda.

I was a deserving gladiator enjoying a feast after an attack in the coliseum by the wild mad beast. After eating every morsel in the can, I threw the can and bottle to the front onto the floor. I would have to bury them after I slept because the smell of food would be inviting to animals. I covered up using the different clothes as blankets. The dog bite itched but did not stop me from falling into a deep, deep sleep, dreaming about a world where life hadn't changed for years.

CHAPTER SIX

It was a cold night. I hadn't moved and slept a long time. The food, hike to the house, and fight with the dogs had exhausted me. I was between sleep and consciousness. I needed all the rest I could get so I would be ready for the next adventure.

A disturbance was pulling at me, challenging my senses so staying asleep was impossible. It hadn't been there when I slipped into the car. I heard dragging sounds. I woke up remembering how the dogs had snuck up on me. That memory put me on guard. I opened my eyes, grabbed the staff, held still, and listened.

If it were those dogs again, I wouldn't spare them a second time. I felt anger rising in my body. I heard my pulse pumping in my ears as if I'd just finished a long run. It was dark and scary. I sat up staring into blackness. Something was moving around and created a shuffling sound. The dogs have returned and were on top trying to dig their way into my sanctuary, I thought. If they had followed my scent, I would see one of them in the window soon. Maybe, they were waiting to jump on me the next time I left. I heard a small cry. It sounded more human than dog. I jumped into the front seat to peer out the front window. The darkness and open hood made it impossible.

I opened the glove compartment and found the matches. Then I poked my staff out the open passenger window to see if there would be any reaction to it. Nothing happened. I pushed myself out head first keeping my staff in front of me. I lay there for a second, halfway expecting a critter to jump from the roof. Nothing happened, so I kept sliding out. I stood up, stayed down low behind the car, and peered over the roof. My ears felt stretched out. Again, I heard shuffling and another soft whimper. This thing was close. I moved towards the noise, still holding my staff in front. This wasn't a dog returning. It was another human.

Whatever was moving around seemed to be wandering aimlessly, not straight towards me or straight away. I imagined someone with shoes on not paying attention to clumps of mud and holes. A painful sounding cry followed each tripping noise. I had no flashlight, candle, or anything. A match would shine light on me, making me dangerously visible while not showing me much. I closed my eyes to see if I could use my surprise powers. Nope, nothing was there to help.

Closer and closer, I moved towards the sound. A breeze brought the stinky smell from the stumbler. It was definitely strong body odor. It had to be a person or large animal because there had been no bushes or trees standing as tall. I got close enough to see the stumbling figure.

This person wasn't big. Whoever it was, hadn't noticed me. I yelled, "Hey." No response came. I yelled again, but still the walker did not stop. Something was wrong. We were getting farther away from the car walking in circles. I worried about finding my way back. I moved in right behind the prowler. The smell was pungent. Couldn't let the stink stop me or worry me. This encounter was too important to abandon.

With one hand, I grabbed a shoulder and twirled him

around so he faced me. He was frail and easy to pull. I kept the staff across my chest. I lit a match. The breeze blew it out. Even so, it was enough to allow me a glimpse. It was a young black girl. She was sick or in shock. I couldn't clearly see her face. The torn and burned blouse barely covered her. "Who, who are you?" I stuttered. No answer came back. I stuck my face up close to hers. She was older than I was. I guessed fifteen or sixteen. What should I do? I couldn't leave her out there wandering. She would fall into a hole or become dog food for sure. It wasn't the right thing to do. I had to take care of her. I tugged her by the hand and led her back to the car. She was easy to direct, except she kept stumbling on the smallest of lumps. I felt her weakness. She had long hair but something was strange.

I pushed her head through the window onto the front seat. Putting my hands on her back, I shoved her farther. She slid flat on her stomach without a peep. This was the best place for her in her condition. Sharing the backseat would have been hard with someone in her condition. I threw my staff over the backseat so it would be close. I mentally marked its location.

Making sure not to step on her, I crawled in the window and crossed over her. I jumped into the backseat and dug through my stack of clothes. I took a few large pieces out, unbundled them, and laid them across her backside to keep her warm. I hoped when I woke up she'd still be there and the rest of this night would pass peacefully. She was in no shape to answer any of my questions. I went to sleep.

When I awoke, something was different. It was brighter outside. At least, I could tell the difference between night and day. My staff was still in front of me. Before sitting up, I listened for sounds. Hearing nothing different, I sat up and leaned over the seat. There she was. I watched her back to see if she was breathing. I saw her ribs expand. She hadn't moved all night. Her legs were brown and covered with sticky sand. I reached down and touched her shoulder softly, but she had no reaction. I could see why her hair had looked funny. It was black and hung down over one shoulder. One side of her head was bald like mine. She must have had protection on one side when the burning air hit her. I could see her bald side was red down to her neck, like the burns on my body.

I returned the loose clothes to the rear seat. She ignored me. I took her legs and turned her lower body sideways. I hooked my arm under her shoulder and rolled her chest and head over.

She was facing me. She was awake but her open eyes stared far, far away. I dug down on the floor, found a bottle of water, and laid it on her legs. I climbed over the seat. I straddled her by putting my knee on the seat beside her and the other foot on the floorboard. Placing my hands under her armpits, I pulled her up with all my strength. It took two tries, but finally she was sitting up against the door so I could pour water in her mouth. I pulled down gently on her chin to get her mouth open. I opened the sport bottle. Holding her chin down, I squirted water into her mouth. She gagged a little but then swallowed. She drank half a bottle. I tore open one of my precious packs of M & M's, put one in her mouth. It just sat there in her mouth. She wasn't ready to eat.

I realized I had inherited a big problem. This was another human, I didn't know, drinking my water. To top it off, she would be no help in finding more food or water. I couldn't get a word out of her. No matter how much I yelled or whispered in her ear, she didn't change her blank stare. I gave her more water in the afternoon and crushed M & M's. She drank water but still didn't eat. This was her first day with me. I couldn't leave her there alone because it wouldn't be safe.

It would be stupid to explore in another direction with someone so handicapped and slow. This day was hers. I talked to her even though she didn't react. I told her about the dogs, the house, and the collapsed building. Describing the bugs and bodies didn't get a reaction. She took none of it in, but my feelings of loneliness seemed to wane.

It was too much for me to stay put. Besides, leaving the car for a small scouting trip around the area wouldn't be too bad. I picked up my treasured staff and slipped out. I first circled the car to check for tracks from others. As I set out, I heard squeaking sounds. Maybe a flock of birds was there. When I reached the other side of a mound, it was shocking. Rats the size of a small dog were everywhere. Their tails were sharp and many of them had burns as I did, making them furless to varying degrees. There were many more on the way. This enormous pack of rats must have flocked together to find food.

My heart sank remembering the helpless girl I'd left in the car. Turning back, I ran as fast as I could to her. I heard shrill screams. Rats had beaten me to her. I saw them on the roof trying to jump into the open window. Some had made it into the backseat. Rat bites must have shocked her back into reality. She was frantically swinging her arms and kicking her feet.

Rats were crawling up from the backseat. One jumped on her chest and bit her. The pain made her scream horribly. Her screams petrified me. The ugly vermin swarmed on the roof.

I ran behind the car, climbed on top, and swung my staff like a golf club. I felt almost superhuman clubbing the crap out of those rodents. One came from behind and nipped my ankle. I jumped off the car and swung at it. It flew in the air and crumpled up on the ground. Others I hit fell victim to their pals. I climbed back up to swing at them again. Making it to the other side I cleared the roof and looked down at the window to help guard it. The girl was doing a good job of keeping them out. I took the staff and stabbed it down hitting the rats on their backs or heads. She couldn't ward them off for much longer. I had to get inside and help her.

I only wanted to kill the ones after the girl. She was hysterical because two of them were on her body. One was near her throat and the other on her stomach close to her thighs. I slid into the front seat and hit the first one hard and watched the blood splash on the seat. She grabbed the other one by the head and battered it against the dash. As they came over from the back, I swatted them. In the backseat, they were chewing the M & M's, paper, and all. I took my staff and smashed each one. By now, the girl had stopped yelling. She was pale white. Her chest was bleeding from bites.

I jumped in the backseat, found my apron bags, and then threw the cans and bottles inside them with the jewelry and bank. I didn't know if I got everything, but we had to move.

Tossing an apron over the front seat, I told her to, "Take it then get out!"

"No," she said.

I screamed, "There are thousands more! They are coming this way." She looked me in the eyes and saw my terror, and then slid out the window, over the dead bleeding rats. She stood and turned towards the window then leaned in to get the apron. Incredibly, two rats jumped from the roof onto her back.

She screamed, then dropped the apron on the seat and quickly slid back into the car. The rats had us trapped. I shouldn't have held things up for the food. I took the dead rats from the backseat and threw them out the window as a distraction for the others. As soon as one left, another appeared. I grabbed the screwdriver and handed it to the girl. She poked forward at the rats as I smashed them as fast as I could. Occasionally, one would get a good bite on my staff and I swung it loose. Lucky for us, the window was the only way into the car. It was hard for them to pass through with both of us fighting them. We could hold our own; I didn't know how long.

These ravenous creatures were not smart like dogs. They only knew one way to fight, nonstop to the death.

The girl yelled, "I can't go on like this." I knew what she meant. A couple rats had slipped into the backseat. I hit them with a can. They were wearing us out. The ones we killed were not enough to distract the horde. Only a miracle could save us.

With splattered blood covering her forearms, the girl poked the rats in the eyes. The smell and taste of blood in the air engaged our primeval defenses. We worked as a tag team. I distracted them with the swinging staff and the newly dead or disabled companions while she reached out and blinded them. We had a system, but it wasn't a pretty sight. We were close to losing the battle and our reaction time was getting slower and slower. More rats kept coming. A couple of them were on the floorboard in front and were raising their paws up to scratch my new partner. I yelled, "Toss the aprons back here." We had lost the front seat.

She straddled the front seat and fell into the back next to me. I watched while the front seat filled up with crazed demons. They were pouring in. I placed my staff horizontally over the seat top and pushed them back. They tried to climb up on it as I was shoving back. I felt the girl next to me. She kept them off my hands and arms with that nasty screwdriver. So far, we were holding the line. Somehow, our coordination came together, our timing was right, but fatigue was taking hold. We were no longer maiming and killing. We hardly kept the wave pushed back. It was a no-win situation.

I closed my eyes. What I saw this time was unbelievable. The back of the car appeared wide open. This vision made little sense. How could there be a way out through the back of my car, my cave, my sanctuary, and my haven? I closed my eyes again and saw the same thing. What did this mean? I yelled at the girl, "Close your eyes and look back." I kept mine focused on the snarling teeth coming over the front seat. She closed her eyes and when she opened them, her face filled with disbelief. How could the car have a way out when we were using it to protect our backs? The girl didn't know about the powers.

A couple more rats jumped onto the backseat floor. They bit into my leg right below where the dog had bitten me. I felt the pain, released the staff, and then thrust my fist down towards them. It wasn't enough. I grabbed the staff again. We couldn't keep defending ourselves. More rats jumped into the backseat. I felt trapped. In those few moments, I lost track of the girl. I closed my eyes after the next bite. To my surprise, a vision of a path heading out through the rear reappeared. "Let's close our eyes and use this way out," I yelled. I kept mine closed while freely crawling out. I could see the ground ahead. I was crawling through solid objects. Once I got outside, I opened my eyes and sprinted away. The horde was too slow to stay with me. I didn't look back. I ran until I dropped. Shortly afterwards, the girl fell next to me. The rats had bitten us all over our legs and arms. During our escape, I hadn't seen the girl grabbing the two aprons. She might turn into a good partner. We had bonded in battle, fought as one and beat the hungry devils back long enough to find a new power, and escape.

I gasped, "Let's keep moving." I tossed an apron over my shoulder, closed my eyes, and envisioned the path back to the house. It wasn't very bright out. Darkness wouldn't matter. I had a power of vision that worked in the light or dark. She followed me not saying a word. The only sound was the cans and bottles knocking together and an occasional grunt from me. The bites on my legs were painful, but I didn't want to stop. I needed something to drink and to eat, but getting away from the rats was more important. We kept going until I heard her ask if we could stop to rest. I didn't hesitate. I was ready to hug the ground. Without a word, I fell face down.

Rolling over, I looked down at my legs and saw why they were itching. The gnats were back, swarming around my wounds. I looked over at the girl. Sprawled out on her back she was staring towards the sky. The bugs were all over her. She had more open wounds than me. I tried to brush the bugs away, but as soon as I would wave them off, they came right back.

Once on a TV nature program, I had watched elephants throw dirt on themselves to keep the flies away. I reached out for the wet mud and dabbed it on my legs and arms. A fine layer stuck and became a shield. It hurt when I touched right on the bites, but I stopped flinching after a few times. The girl saw what I was doing and imitated me. Other than the bugs being close to our faces and mouths as irritants, we were free from them.

After a few minutes, I heard her say she was thirsty. I opened my apron, found a bottle of water, and told her, "Drink slowly." I passed her a bag of M & M's. She gobbled up all of them. It was like watching ravenous rats eat. At least, she threw the paper aside. This was the first time we'd been together conscious and secure. Our immediate mission was to get away from the man-eating horde of rats, find shelter, and more food and drink.

We were too tired and panicked to socialize but one other thing was bothering me. I had to know her name. It was awkward being so personally close to her and not know her name. I looked over as she was resting and noticed her wounds covered with mud and her half a head of hair.

I asked, "What's your name?"

"Kelly Kathleen or KK for short. And yours?"

"Brock." She repeated it and it sure sounded good hearing it from someone else. I used the opportunity to mention my "Take it slow and be careful" motto.

Our car sanctuary had become a haven for rats. There were only two known places to go: the buried building area or the house stuck in the bank of mud. The house was the best choice. I might have stayed there on my first visit if my food supply hadn't been back at the car. This time I had food plus company.

CHAPTER SEVEN

We didn't speak the entire distance. She didn't know where we were going and strangely enough, she didn't ask. When we reached the house, KK stopped in front. I guess she couldn't believe her eyes. We entered quickly. With the light fading outside, I stayed on the first floor in case we'd have to escape another threat. I showed KK the invisible stairs and informed her that the clothes we left back at the car had come from this house.

I showed her the room where I had left women's clothing on my earlier visit. She'd need something to stay warm. She picked out a long blouse. It was for an adult just as my shirt was. She slipped it on and returned to the hallway. Oversized shirts were a lot easier to keep on than ill-fitted trousers. We appeared to be runaways from a lunatic pajama party. We found the bedroom with the double bed in it. KK helped me pull the mattress over to the stairwell. One large white thick blanket was a comforter. Even though it was filthy, I could still see a blue floral design. We took anything of use downstairs where escape wouldn't involve jumping out of a two-story window. In the bathroom, we found the stool with the lid down. I worried KK would have the same urge I had before and want to use it. I explained the deposit was mine so she wouldn't be worried. We found small things like hair rollers with picks, one small bar of soap, and two washcloths. We had explored all three bedrooms. KK commented, "Someone else could have been to the house before us and taken the useful things."

We shimmied down the invisible stairs and jumped down onto the waiting mattress. We needed a solid room for our new hideout with an exit via a window or door. The dining room had a large missing bay window. It was also large enough to shelter us from any wind or rain during storms. We pulled the mattress over to the highest dry corner, grabbed the big blanket, and spread it out. KK retrieved the aprons with our precious food and drinks and put them in full view on the mattress edge. Without me suggesting it, she knew we should have this stuff close by.

We went up next to the wall and sat down on the mattress with no pillows around to cushion the hard wall. We had inherited a hard place but we assembled a comfortable nest. To celebrate, I opened the first bottle of soda. It was a generic cola. Regardless, it tasted better than any sip of cola I'd ever had. I took a big gulp and passed it to KK. When she passed it back, I finished it. I dug down into one pouch for another pack of M & M's but found none.

I asked, "Can you find more M & M's?"

"No M & M's left."

I found the can of sardines, picked up the screwdriver, and poked holes in the top. I pried on the holes until the tin tore to the next hole. The top was uncovered; enough to get the oily fish out. Some other food would've tasted better, but I had a habit of saving the best for last whenever I ate a meal. Saving the small sweet green peas for last was a reward for having eaten all the other things you didn't like.

The sardines were all gone.

While dabbing the oil off our hands with washcloths,

I asked her, "Where are you from?"

"Mullins Road."

"Mullins Road is not far from my home on Flecher Street."

She didn't seem to recognize it.

"How were we able to escape the car?"

"It must be from whatever created this catastrophe." I wasn't sure she shared the same new powers. I explained how the visions of seeing where we had been worked.

"Close your eyes to see the trail back to the car." Intuitively, she looked toward the car's location and closed her eyes. She saw the trail. I explained, "The visions started when I left this house on my first visit, the rain had washed away my trail." We both agreed it was unbelievable and wondered what else we might discover. KK named the visions "look-feels."

Next, I warned her about wild animals. I reinforced the warning by describing how the dogs had attacked me.

She asked, "Where did you get the food?" That led me to describe the two trips to the restaurant. I again mentioned the motto I had adopted and said that we both needed to follow it. She didn't seem to have a problem with the command position I had taken.

She asked, "How did you find me?" I described the scary dark encounter when she showed up shuffling around.

I added, "I couldn't let you roam deliriously in the dark where wild dangerous animals or deep holes were sure to take your life."

KK described her family life, "I am an army brat. My father is a sergeant in the army and he always took us with him except for two short tours in Korea. We lived in Germany, France, and five states. My father runs our home like an army base by shouting out orders."

I exclaimed, "Wow, I've never traveled anywhere. I have never left the state. My parents are divorced and I live with my mother."

"How much time do you spend with your father?"

"I see him every other weekend and one week in the summer for a camping trip." We had something in common, absentee fathers.

She was accustomed to starting over. Compared to her, I had led a mundane existence.

Darkness had fallen. We covered up and fell asleep. We were sharing a growing fellowship driven by fear, loneliness, and the unknown.

I woke up first. I rolled off the mattress trying not to wake her, but it didn't work. Reaching into an apron, I slipped a bottle of water out and passed it to her.

I let her know, "It is yours to nurse."

She drank some, and then commented, "This tastes great." I found another bottle and took sips. The sardine taste made my mouth taste like rotten meat. It became clearer after KK sent a whiff of her breath my way.

Oddly, I wondered what day it was. In the old world, it was something you had to know, but here it was of no consequence. It had to be one of many old useless habits. All that mattered was survival. It was that simple. It was simpler than the world KK bounced around with her family. Personal survival and confrontation were all that mattered, and it was up to us.

KK's needs would cut my supplies in half. The rats had eaten their share. We needed to take inventory of our food. KK opened her apron and dumped it all out. I dumped mine. It didn't look good at all. My guess was that we had enough for five days at most. There were three sodas and one bottle of water.

I let her know, "The supplies should last five days."

She said, "What then?"

I explained, "We can start by going on a scouting trip like I did from the car, walking the opposite direction from my original approach." She agreed with the approach.

We prepared for our scouting trip. I found curtain cords hanging from busted window frames and used them as a belt. I put the screwdriver in the belt and grabbed an empty apron to take along for the trip. We had already stored the food in a closet. KK kept her bottle of water and I did, too. We blocked the closet door with the big chair.

We climbed over the bay window sill in the dining room and fell to the ground. We stopped for a moment to get our bearings. We glanced back at the trail leading towards the car, turned the opposite direction, and began our adventure. I explained my step counting measuring system to KK. She suggested we take turns counting. Then I realized something had just changed. KK had contributed to our progress for the first time with her suggestion. Although it was a small contribution, it was the first time she added to an activity unless you count saving the aprons. I enjoyed being in control. I knew she may take over and regretfully, I would relent.

We didn't talk while walking. We had to keep our full attention on counting. I believe it was around 4,000 steps when we ran into trouble. Everything ahead looked the same as behind us. No sign of life. No sign of buildings, cars, trees, nothing. KK led the way while moving fast to avoid being a target. She probably weighed less than I weighed but was taller. She had long legs with well-defined calves. I skipped once in a while to keep up.

Predators search for the weak, old, and sick. We were none of those. I envisioned a wave of fear in front of us where all possible threats would recognize our presence and back away. My confidence was at its peak.

I heard a loud crashing sound and watched KK's head lowering down as if she was on an escalator. After she was out of sight, the ground under me slowly gave out. KK disappeared in a cloud of dust that came shooting up like splashed water. Without warning, my nose filled with dirt and my mouth became coated with dust. I didn't know how far I fell. My head struck something hard. I was nearly unconscious.

KK didn't suffer the same fate. She stayed conscious. I stayed dead still for ten minutes. The fall left me fuzzy headed. I could hardly hear her.

She called, "Brock, Brock, help!"

My body felt like a truck had hit it. My head had a big throbbing bump on it. I rolled over towards KK's calls. I heard her clearly and felt the panic in her voice.

As we fell, we went in opposite directions.

I yelled to KK, "I'm okay and I'll be right there." My makeshift belt was off and the screwdriver was gone. I saw my apron as I looked towards KK. She still held hers.

As fast as I could, I got to her side. She was lying flat out with her foot twisted under a heavy beam. When she tried to move or break loose, it hurt worse. With difficulty, she could sit up. I grabbed the exposed end and tried to lift it. It was impossible. Looking around, I saw a broken concrete block and three long boards still nailed together. I went over, put my foot on the bottom board, and pried the top one off. The board would work well as a pry bar if it didn't break. I used the block as a fulcrum and placed the board's end under the beam. I warned KK to be ready to free her foot.

She yelled, "Okay already." The pain put her on edge. I pushed down with my hands to raise the beam. It hardly moved. Still, it was enough to make KK scream out when it jiggled. KK glared at me. I sat on the end, slowly letting my weight raise the beam. That did the trick. KK's foot was free. I ran for a can of soda and gulped it down. The fall's impact and the hurt from my bruised body hadn't caught up with me. I had ignored it to rescue KK.

KK attempted to get up but failed. Her foot was too sore to stand on. She and I had been part of a building's collapse. It may have been the right time for it to go or most likely, our combined weight triggered it. Whatever the reason, we quit. We had to return to the house so KK could rest and heal. Her foot couldn't support her. I collected the aprons and then reached down and pulled

KK up on her good foot. She kept her knee bent and hopped on one foot. I looked around the hole and found the easiest wall to climb. KK climbed up leading the way. After we reached the top, she used me as a crutch for the trip back to the house. Her sore foot barely touched the ground as she stepped forward. Once we found a rhythm, it was easier. We had to stop two times to rest. When the house came into view, the relief gave me more energy. It had been a tedious half-mile with KK leaning on me. I helped her back into the house where she crawled onto the mattress. She laid down, covered up, and promptly went to sleep. Being tired, but not sleepy, I sat next to her. For a while, we were safely back in the house.

CHAPTER EIGHT

My stomach growled from hunger. I went for a can of food. I couldn't believe my eyes! It wasn't how we left it. Something or someone had pushed the chair aside. The closet door was partially open. Alarm bells went off in my head. Someone had invaded our house while we scouted for food. I backed away, not wanting to turn my back on whatever might be there. I was ready to run at any sign of danger. Slowly, I returned to KK. I needed to protect her. Keeping my eyes focused on the closet, I jumped on the mattress and moved close to KK. To wake her up, I nudged her. When she moved, I told her, "Be quiet."

She whispered, "What's wrong?"

"We might be in danger; the closet door is open."

She stiffened up with a wince of pain. I didn't know what to do.

She suggested, "Get as close to the closet without being seen and listen for movement."

I tiptoed back, slowly moving closer and closer, hoping the old floor wouldn't make creaking noises. There was no movement, breathing, or growling. My interest piqued, I had to discover what was behind the door. I reached the door and attempted to look through the crack in between the hinges. It was of no use. I couldn't see anything. If I moved the door, I would've given away my presence. I went right to the edge and did a quick bob of my head around the opening snapping a mental picture. I wasn't sure what was there and repeated the peek-a-boo move. Finally, I just stood in front of it. It was empty. Whoever had been there, had taken our food. KK was watching me.

I hurried back to her and quietly whispered, "Nothing was there."

"Do you think they're still here?"

"I hope not!"

KK spoke up, "There is enough light outside to see tracks around the house. You should scout around the house to find any traces of visitors."

I didn't feel like she was trying to boss me around because I hadn't a clue what to do. If I had been alone, I would've just ran off.

She said, "I will watch you through different windows and shout out a warning if anything pops up." She instructed me to move slowly, so she'd have time to crawl to each side and work her way up to the windows. Out the front door, I jumped to the ground. I kept close to the outside wall so I wouldn't be out in the open. If I had to retreat, it would be back inside with KK. I looked side to side for tracks. Ours were the only tracks. I walked around the corner. I saw KK make it to the window to watch me. No tracks were evident except for the ones from us jumping out. Turning the corner again, I saw no tracks at all. With one side left, I paused so KK could make it to her next lookout window. I expected to see tracks past the next corner. I stepped around and the ground was void of any marks. What could this mean? We didn't move the chair or take the cans. No one but us had left tracks. Shrugging my shoulders, I looked at the house. KK was leaning against a hole that used to be a window. I saw the second floor glassless windows.

Looking up farther, I saw something I had previously missed. This house had small windows above the bedrooms for an attic. I hadn't found doors or stairs to the attic when I searched the upstairs. This had to be the answer. Underneath the house, you'd only find the mud that pushed it here. I pointed toward the attic. KK stuck her head out and peered upward. I headed for the front door. When I reached KK, I whispered, "I believe someone is in the attic." She hobbled back to the safety of our mattress.

KK couldn't make it up the invisible stairs with her injured foot. I had to investigate. I went upstairs and found nothing in the first bedroom. I entered the other room where the floor looked unsafe. It had a closet door in the corner. The attic stairs had to be there. "Yes!"

The first step to the attic crackled from my weight. I kept going regardless. I reached the top. Looking around I noticed blankets, old boxes and beside them, our stolen cans, but no culprit. A large crooked chimney was the only notable feature. I moved towards the cans and closer to the chimney. I saw who it was. It was a young skinny kid, younger and shorter than I was. He appeared to be nine or ten years old with buckteeth and bushy curly hair. He had no burns. His clothes were still intact. He was wearing black shorts with a gray sweatshirt. He was barefoot. When I spotted him, he jumped back away towards the broken window.

"You don't have to be afraid of me," I said. He kept moving backwards. I reached down for a can. I said, "You can have this. It's okay." He nodded his head no. He didn't risk coming close. Maybe my cuts, bites, scratches, burns, and bald head put him on edge. Whatever it was, I didn't need to rush the situation.

I said, "My name is Brock. What's yours?"

He stood silent for a few minutes. Then, with a slight stutter, he said, "T-Tim." We had each other's name.

"How long have you been here?"

"I don't know."

"Did you see me the first time I was here?"

"Yes."

I assumed he'd been in this house since doom-night. While we were out fighting animals and elements, Tim was there staying snug. Yet, Tim seemed terrified, even if he hadn't faced all our earlier trials.

Tim moved closer. I asked, "What have you been eating?" He pointed to the boxes. I looked in them. Empty wrappers that included an empty box of macaroni and cheese, health bar wrappers, and two cereal boxes hung all over them. He pulled the cereal boxes out to reveal more cans. There were three cans of green beans and four cans of soup. None opened.

I asked, "What plans do you have when you run out of food?"

Tim said, "Don't know."

KK and I were no better off. Our hunt away from the house may never provide us with more food.

Tim had gathered up the food. I then asked, "Where is your water?" He pointed towards a window. There, sitting in the dark, I could make out a big plastic water jug. I walked over to it and found a small cup right beside it. I asked, "Can I have a drink." He nodded his head yes. After the drink, I looked around for anymore goodies but saw nothing.

I asked, "Do you want to come downstairs with us?" He didn't answer right away. I followed with, "We'd be happy to have you." It was a cinch he wouldn't make it on his own.

Tim said, "Okay."

Tim took one box and put the blankets in it, carried it down the attic stairs, out to the hall and threw it down the fallen stairwell. It made a big bang when it hit causing a cloud of dust. I grabbed the other box and followed him. My mind flashed to KK and how she would feel about a surprise bang like that. I yelled downstairs, "Everything is okay." Once the food, water, and supplies were safely down, Tim shimmied down the stairwell and finished with a long jump to the bottom. He seemed reckless, but he was younger than I was. I led him into the room where KK was sitting. As he came around the corner, KK's eyes lit up. It was as if she'd seen an old friend. The relief from not having a dangerous demon in the attic and the sight of this cute small boy must have let her forget her troubles for a moment. I thought I saw just a glimpse of a smile.

I said, "Tim this is Kelly Kathleen or KK for short."

Tim said, "My name is Tim Walker."

"Happy to meet you," KK said.

Tim shyly smiled back but did not answer. I let KK know he had our food and water and more. She stopped smiling and became serious. I could see the wheels turning in her head.

CHAPTER NINE

Tim and I straightened out the items we had thrown down the staircase while KK spent time resting and thinking.

After a long pause she blurted out, "Devil's Bend, Devil's Bend!"

I didn't understand what she meant. I asked, "What's Devil's Bend?"

"Devil's Bend is a curve in the river where it loops around side-by-side. My dad is in charge of a shelter there. It's unknown to the public and is exclusively for government officials and their families. My dad is in charge of the guards." She mentioned maintenance crews with supplies flown in by helicopter. The guards enter during inspections. She described it as a complex of underground buildings, furnished with the best furniture and equipment. It had hot tubs, swimming pools, game rooms, and gym equipment. Her dad had joked, "It is an underground country club and resort with everything except a golf course." They stocked it full of food, enough to supply 200 people for two years.

Her father explained to her if a bomb hit America, the officials would have the first warning and they would rush to this shelter. Rumor was that at least 100 of these existed in the states. Officials never were far away from protection. They made allowances for their extended families to join them and her father had the complete list of all who could enter. The government didn't want every citizen trying to get into them in case of a national emergency. Shelters were in the biggest cities while others were in rural areas like ours. The one her father was guarding was in the woods without roads. Only way in was by helicopter. The government owned the property around it for miles. No one locally was aware it existed.

KK's father wasn't supposed to tell anyone. He had made KK promise to keep it secret, too. He wanted her to know why he was gone so much. His on duty time was eleven days and nights on and eleven days and nights at home. Her father said it took longer to get to the shelter going to the base to catch a flight, than walking straight there through the woods. Once he had pointed towards the big hills by the river, to show where it was.

We couldn't survive on the small supplies we had found. Maybe we'd find gardens or stores that had survived. All that depended on luck. We had to find Devil's Bend. Not knowing where we were, made it hard to imagine ever getting there.

I asked Tim, "What is your address?" He hadn't lived in town but a few miles outside. My instincts told me we were closer to my house. Right or wrong, I guessed we were far away from the hills. I went upstairs and looked out the windows for any signs of civilization or hills. I spotted a big black smoky fire burning but nothing in any other direction. The fire was coming from the direction of our car. The fire was surely a sign that something big was exposed. We had seen nothing like that. Rushing towards the fire could be dangerous, but it was the only sign that some remnant of civilization still existed. We'd have to get up early to find the fire in one day. I explained my plan and why. They nodded their heads in agreement. KK was hurting so much that I could hardly expect any contribution or opinion from her. Tim was the newcomer. I guessed he didn't feel comfortable voting or objecting.

KK said, "How about the rats?"

I replied, "We may need to outrun them again or they may have disbanded or roamed off"

I thought it wasn't the best answer but sometimes to move forward, taking risk was the only answer.

We rested on the big mattress and chatted. KK described strange things she'd experienced in her travels. They exposed her to many customs and different food. I felt a pang of jealousy. She said, "My father was almost ready to retire. He had heard about the open post from a friend. It was just the thing to finish his career, low stress with few responsibilities." Her father had insisted she learn how to use weapons and attend first aid classes. She did not like the gun classes. Loud noises with the dangerous recoil of weapons were not her idea of fun. She went along with it because the other army brats were doing it. It was "expected." Her father had signed her up for marksman contests, but she did so poorly that he was shamed into not pursuing it. KK always believed her father would have rather had a boy instead of a girl. She fought the idea of becoming a soldier. KK didn't have the aggressive nature required to satisfy her father.

Tim sat and listened. He had gotten used to us. Every day he caught a school bus to town. His father and mother were farmers but his dad had been hurt so badly they had to lease the land out. Tim described to us how he'd get up early to get eggs from the chickens, feed the pigs, and sometimes hook the milking machines to their cows. He said his mother would have to do the chores if he didn't. His dad couldn't lift or carry anything. It was hard for his father to walk to the barn from the house. Tim was dedicated. He knew how to work hard. He would be a good addition to my growing troop.

I asked, "Why aren't you burned like KK and me?"

"I don't know."

"What were you doing when the explosion hit?"

"Taking a bath."

The tub and the water protected him from the burning heat wave.

"What happened?"

"I don't know."

"Have you any new powers?" He looked at me as if I was crazy.

"New powers?"

I explained, "KK and I have new things we can do." I explained what they were. He looked at me with bewilderment. He probably wouldn't comprehend what they were until we showed him. We dozed off.

Tim was the first one up in the morning. He was moving a leg up into the air and dropping it. That was enough to wake us. I said, "We have to hide the supplies better than before." We looked around and found a hole in the floor. It wouldn't be as obvious there.

I shimmied up to the second floor and checked on the fire. It looked bigger than before. It would be easy to find. I had Tim get bottles of water and five cans of food. We packed up the aprons. KK's foot was much better but she was still walking with a limp.

We ventured out towards the fire even though nothing visible was at ground level. KK suggested we follow each other at a distance, that way if something caved in, only one person would take a tumble. I took the lead. Tim followed ten steps behind. KK took up the rear. If we kept on the move, we'd arrive soon. My pace was fast until I looked back and saw Tim and KK not able to keep pace. I stopped for a few minutes to let them catch up with me. At least an hour passed before we stopped. I checked on KK's badly bruised foot. Her limp had become less evident. Walking must have deadened the pain. Tim was in good shape. I felt stiff after starting up again, but we all hooked up with a marching cadence and our travel was fast but cautious.

We smelled smoke. We walked for a few miles more. On the top of a small hill, we realized how big the blaze was. Making our way to the upwind side, we figured out what was burning. It was our town.

Half the buildings were smoldering. We sat down to watch the fire eat up what used to be our peaceful village. Tall mud cliffs surrounded the town. It looked like lava flow images I'd seen. The streets and roads that surrounded the center of town where my home and KK's home had been were gone. I looked for signs of people stirring. There were none.

I asked KK, "Do you remember what you were doing during the explosion?" She nodded her head no. We agreed to call it "doom-night."

I had to keep in mind that finding our location in relation to Devil's Bend was the most important task. Once we found something familiar, maybe KK could remember the direction to her home and to the hills. I was counting on it. It was such a small town. We had a supermarket, two gas stations, a coffee shop, city hall, barbershop, a dime store, and one large hardware store with farm equipment. My favorite places were the cafeteria with great desserts and the tiny two room post office. The old lady postmaster, Talie, at the post office had the sweetest smile. The Main Street grain elevator was the tallest structure.

The fire produced nauseous black smoke and stunk like burning rubber. We had a junkyard so maybe the fire was burning the big pile of black tires there. My friends and I used to climb up to the top and look around at old wrecked cars. My mother always complained about the black stains on my clothes from the rubber tires.

The buildings were not in the exact place as we remembered them. Some had shuffled a little, burned, collapsed, or were cloaked in smoke.

We couldn't tell north from south, east from west. Without sun or stars, it was impossible to figure out directions in such a devastated location. We climbed down the newborn mud cliff. There were streets filled with debris. They were the safer places to walk without having to jump over parts of burned-out buildings. We could see sections of buildings and houses where one wall or a chimney stood upright. There were gray puffs of smoke from hot embers flowing through the air. Crackling sounds from burning and settling buildings came from every direction.

I had an eerie feeling as if we had landed on an alien planet. I imagined an alien would rise and attack us with his giant space torch.

Surely, we should have seen bodies. Aloud I asked, "Where are the people?" We found a car in the middle of the road. I looked inside. There in the front seat rested the blackened remains of a person. It blended in with the charred car as if it all was one. Dried out black remnants of townspeople were buried in these buildings or in the mounds of blown trash. They were as crispy as burned toast. Bugs and rodents would pass on them because they wouldn't make a meal. My idea suspecting aliens didn't seem so far-fetched when faced with this cinder pit.

KK looked disgusted and bewildered, "Why?" she asked. Tim didn't fully comprehend the situation. He seemed awestruck by it all. After seeing the body, we knew what to look for. As we walked along, we spotted more but not many.

Each time Tim spied one he yelled out, "There's one!" Sometimes he yelled when it wasn't one. He made it a game.

The fire was still raging at the other end of town. It was far enough away to pose no danger. We had to stay focused. As we turned the corner, we spotted a big US mailbox lying on the pavement. The familiar blue post office colors were gone. It had been so hot that the paint burned off, leaving it a rusty red color. This was our clue. We had reached Main Street. Our town only had one outside mailbox and it was in front of our small post office. We had found our anchor.

I asked KK, "Do you know where we are now?" She looked at the mailbox, and nodded her head yes. Without hesitation, she pointed above the fire towards the hills her father had designated.

"Do you want to go there right now?"

"What else?"

"We might find water and food first," KK still bowed to my wishes.

"Fine." She trusted me to be the leader.

Tim wasn't paying attention. He was still playing "find the body game" but with little luck. I couldn't count on him for counsel or direction. I wanted to find Bishop's Cafeteria.

My first supplies were from a buried building. Maybe I could be lucky in another one. We passed small burned buildings. The cafeteria had been a long building. We passed a few with basements where the first floor had collapsed into the hole. The fourth building didn't have a basement. The fire burned it almost flat to the ground. It was long enough to be Bishop's. I stepped out on the burned floor. KK and Tim stayed back. I had to be careful not to trip on the charred beams that lay everywhere. I wanted to identify the building. There were different pieces of angled metal. Those could have been from the tables. Then I noticed a tin shelf piece. Pulling it up, I found an almost perfect row of small perfume bottles. This was the dime store. I had found the cosmetic counter that was always so smelly from different concoctions on display. I was in the wrong store so I backed out carefully. The next place had to be Bishop's.

We moved together to the next building. It was tougher because it had a basement. The upper structure had fallen into it. Partially burned collapsed walls and roof covered the sides. To find food, someone would have to climb into the basement.

I asked KK, "Can you do it with your sore feet?"

"Yep." She didn't hesitate. She found a clear area, hung her body down, and dropped. When she landed, she fell back on a beam, which made black soot marks on her shirt, hands, legs, and butt. She rubbed her forehead leaving a black mark on her face. In less than five minutes, she resembled everything else in the hole.

She found nothing useable. I pointed her towards a high spot where the fallen roof wasn't completely broken. On the way there, she found empty bottles and held them up to show us. When she reached the high area, she pulled debris back to see what was underneath. Looking on with apprehension, I couldn't tell what it was, but KK had stopped. She just stood there staring. We couldn't see much in front of her. An upright door blocked our view. I guessed it was metal freezer door. That much we could see. I felt my look-feel. It was strange.

I asked Tim, "What is she doing?"

"Maybe she is afraid?"

I yelled, "What's going on?"

She turned, giving me the come here sign with her arm, and yelled, "Come here, come here!"

I ordered Tim to stay put. I went to the same spot KK had used to get down, hung from the side, and jumped to the bottom. KK had me both worried and excited. What had she found? Was it good or bad? Food or water? Maybe it was money. Money! Money wouldn't be any good in this place. Maybe it was a tunnel? I followed the same path she took. I kicked away the empty bottles. When I got next to her, she moved aside. There, close to the door was a woman. She had black hair and tan complexion resembling a Mexican or Italian. She was leaning against a freezer. The woman didn't talk but motioned for a drink. She looked weak, near death. She must have worked at the cafeteria. Her name tag read Maria. The freezer and basement most likely protected her from the explosion and fire. Heat and lack of food and water had taken its toll.

KK took off to get water. When she reached Tim and let him in on what she had found, Tim threw a partially filled bottle of water down to her. KK recklessly rushed back and scratched her thigh on a nail. She paused for a second to check it out.

Tipping the bottle on her dry lips let the water flow. I gave her small sips each time, waiting for her to swallow.

Maria wasn't a small person; we couldn't carry her all the way on our planned journey. If we left Maria, she would die without more care. It wasn't much of a decision. We had to spend the night nursing her.

I asked KK, "Would you mind staying with Maria while Tim and I search more buildings?" I was sure we'd find something in town.

"No problem."

In the next few hours, if we found supplies, we could feed Maria and ourselves.

I struggled to climb up a beam to make it to the top and return to Tim.

I informed Tim, "We are staying the night in town."

"No, I don't want to!"

"What do you want then?" I didn't give Tim a chance to argue or discuss. I walked away, without looking back. He stayed back standing on the edge of a burned out building.

It didn't take long for him to come running after me saying, "I changed my mind." I acted as if I didn't care and kept moving. Tim stayed with me.

I knew where to find the supermarket. I was after water and canned goods. Once we arrived, I tried to recall where the different foods had been. Fruits and vegetables had been on the left. Canned goods and water had been in the middle or to the right. All shelving had collapsed. At the rear, I saw parts of low freezers that use to be against a wall.

I asked Tim, "Do you want to look for metal cans and

glass bottles?"

"Okay."

"Step lightly. There could be weak floors."

Shopping carts in front had rusty wires. The wheels had just the metal rims because the plastic or rubber wheels had melted. Cash registers were on the floor apart from one another. They were badly burned but recognizable.

Tim soon hit pay dirt. He yelled, "I found them!" He was excited. This was the first time he had done anything useful since we discovered him in the attic. He had found hundreds of cans with labels burned off and many had exploded from heat. The heat had expanded the seams. Finding the cans meant the water was off to the right. Tim came with me to dig out bottles of water. We made it to where the bottles of water had been. The plastic bottles were indistinguishable. The partially filled glass bottles had plastic lids burned off. I had Tim stack them together in one place. I found more glass bottles with metal caps but most had blown their tops from the boiled water. Three out of twenty were in perfect condition.

We had water and plenty of food. Tim was busy finding the partially filled bottles and pouring them together. I went to the cans and carried as many as I could to the front. I piled the first load on the road outside and then grabbed a noisy shopping cart. Worst of all, it didn't want to go straight. I had to keep tugging in one direction to get to the clear spot in the street. I yelled at Tim, "Bring out the water." It would take him at least three trips to get it all. I went back in for more cans. Tim finished with the water and came over to help. We traveled back and forth, not saying a word. Climbing over and ducking under stuff was tough work. Our pace was slow and careful. Tim pulled out another cart. We partially filled it. It was getting late, and we had to get back to Maria and KK. Tim took the emptier cart and I took the filled one. We got behind the carts, pushing them as straight as we could. The metal wheels on the pavement supporting a heavy load made the rattling noises worse. Tim enjoyed the commotion and acted as if he wanted to race. I was too tired and didn't give in to his challenges. I wanted to drink water, eat, and sleep.

When we reached Bishop's basement, I didn't see KK. She must be down there somewhere. I took a bottle of sealed up water and rolled it down into the basement. Our earlier tracks to Maria were evident on the floor and timbers. Tim grabbed a can of food and followed me. He kept close. KK wasn't there. Maria had her eyes closed. "Maria," I whispered. Why I whispered I do not know. I guess I was afraid she was dead. Maria turned towards me with a small smile. This was a good sign. She had gotten better. I asked if she wanted more water and she tried to answer but couldn't. I took the bottle and gave her two small sips. She needed food. Tim had the can of food. Neither of us knew what it was. I found a large nail on a board and pried a hole in the top. It turned out to be a can of sliced green beans with lots of water. I filled up the water bottle with the juice from the beans. I turned the can so the beans would slide out. I couldn't use my black sooty hands to feed someone else. I positioned the can over Maria's mouth. With two beans in her mouth, she chewed ever so slowly. She looked much more alive. The water brought her back. With a few days of care, she'd be back on her feet.

Tim stayed with Maria. I had to find KK. I went back to the large beam we used to climb up and when I reached the top, I saw KK across the street. It must have been the hardware store. KK had already found useful things and was holding them in her hand. I yelled, "Why did you go over there?" She raised her hands showing me hunting knives with handles burned off. I went to KK. She suggested we stay and search for more. So, I dug around, too. I found a whistle that still worked but sounded weird. There were burned shoe soles with no tops and shotguns with burned off handles. I found no unused bullets or shells for the guns. KK found a charred Swiss Army Knife.

Maria and Tim were waiting for our return. KK and I crossed the street. I grabbed another bottle of water. KK put five cans of food in an apron. We had kept the knives for protection. We climbed back down.

Maria was looking better. KK gave Tim the Swiss Army Knife to open cans. It would be another surprise meal. We finished the green beans from before. I ate from the first can and passed it to KK. Tim opened cans of corn, pork and beans, and tomato soup. We passed the cans around and even drank the wicked tasting cold tomato soup. After Tim ate a couple mouthfuls of corn, he tried to feed Maria by tipping the can up to her mouth. He didn't realize he was giving her too much. She spit it out. Dinner was over, yet we were still hungry.

It was twilight. The air had cooled. We had to prepare for the night. That meant clearing space in the basement so we could all stay together. We used short boards to clear off the dirt on the basement floor. I stacked boards around the freezer to shelter us. KK pitched in. We stacked enough boards on top of one another to stop any wind from passing through. Tim sat and watched. We finished our makeshift hut. No one could see us from the street. It was still dusty with soot, but the big pieces of glass and wood were outside.

Our efforts had closed off the world except for one small hole for an exit. Our combined breathing was enough to keep the place a little warmer. Tim snuggled up close to Maria's right side to keep her warm. KK sat next to her other side. I sat closest to the entrance, next to KK.

I had a vision about how Maria would be in good shape when we woke her. We walked towards the hills. KK led the way with Tim and Maria following. I guarded the rear. A light coming from the fort was shining on everyone in front, making halos around their heads. These fantasies were comforting. I fell asleep. The night was cold. As I slept, I felt the air come streaming in from the uncovered entrance. My skin felt like leather, but it didn't stop the cold. I kept my hands down towards my tightly pinched inner thighs to help stay warm.

When I woke up, I felt beaten up and stiff. Everyone was starting to stir. That is, everyone except Maria. Tim had his hand on her forehead. He looked at us and shook his head. I checked her pulse at the neck and felt nothing. I put my cheek by her mouth and nose to detect breathing. Maria had died. We had found her too late. Her death saddened us.

CHAPTER TEN

I sent Tim to check on the shopping carts. KK and I pulled Maria flat to the floor and placed loose boards over her. She hadn't died alone. Maria may have been better off than KK, Tim, and me. We still had to face the unknown outside world and the changes inside of us.

I could still close my eyes and trace my tracks back to any place. KK could do the same. We learned if we pictured a prior destination the path would appear.

Still, Tim had shown no powers. We didn't mention the changes. It was something we hardly understood. Lately, I felt something else different. It was a sensation of presence. I described to KK the feeling in my chest when someone was near. I first felt it when I saw KK looking down at Maria then when she was in the hardware store. The direction made a difference. I felt it right then with her standing close to me. With her, it was a good sensation like when someone close to you hugs you tightly. I expected she'd have it soon.

We started back to meet with Tim. He was sitting down waiting for us. He gave me a strange smile when I looked at him. It wasn't his usual doltish smile but kind of mysterious and serious look.

I asked KK, "Which way?" She walked towards the big fire. Tim took his cart. I pushed the filled one. I turned in different directions while walking down Main Street, trying to feel if there were any other survivors. I felt nothing and assumed no one else had survived. If the explosion didn't kill them, smoke and fire could have finished them. We were alone, well-supplied with a plan.

We reached the end of town where the high ridged mudflows began. The carts were of no further use. I grabbed the water. Tim chose food and KK picked out one of each. We left the carts there and climbed the twenty-foot mud wall. Once we were on top, KK led the way. It was a miracle that her limp was gone.

KK was setting a fast pace. We resumed our marching mode, quietly, watchful, while moving as one unit. We must have walked several hours before we reached the hills. Mud had flowed around them. We reached solid ground on the first hill and found no entry to a complex. The mud could have covered the fences and landing pods. Tim spotted another hill in the same direction. He pointed towards the hill and said, "That's gotta be it there." It was too early to turn back. We had to keep going to find the complex. We trotted over to the other hill. We felt hopeless when we reached the top and still saw no sign of a complex. There were no other hills. KK sprawled out on the ground to rest. Tim sat watching me.

I yelled at Tim to help and he gave me a look of hurt mixed with anger. He scooted down the hill in the opposite direction of our arrival. Almost at the bottom, he yelled, "Brock, I found something!" KK sat up and rolled over to look down at him. I scrambled down to see it. It resembled a manhole cover. It had no identifying marks on it. This had to be a vent or escape hatch. It probably wasn't the only one. It was a big thing made of iron with a pry hole for a bar. We had nothing around strong enough to open it.

We left our provisions except for one bottle of water

on the cover and started our march back to town. It would take a couple hours or more to walk back to town for pry bars.

From the moment we arrived in town, my chest had the slightest pulling. We stopped at our abandoned carts for a drink and left them by the mud cliff. As we moved closer to the center of town, my look-feel grew stronger. KK was feeling something, too. Out there somewhere were humans. It could be one or more. We both sensed them. KK finally had what I had, the power to recognize the nearness of others. Our power of look-feel was growing.

We stopped to plan our next move. Tim looked bewildered by our conversation.

I noted, "They could be dangerous." KK agreed.

I asked, "What direction?" She pointed towards the flattened supermarket. Someone was searching for food just like us.

I asked Tim, "Can you go back to the carts to guard them and our trail back?" Tim needed to be out of harm's way.

"How long will you be?"

KK said, "Not long." Tim left for the carts.

I yelled out to him, "If we don't come back tonight, stay put."

KK and I had proven ourselves in battle before and we had the powers. Whoever was out there could be friend or foe. We had to find a spot that gave us the advantage of our powers. There wasn't much cover. We used the alley behind the buildings across the street from the supermarket. Keeping low, we moved behind one upright structure to another. We were still visible when we hid behind slender shields. Once we got almost straight across from them, we dropped flat.

We heard three voices. They were cussing repeatedly. We spotted them rummaging through a burned store. They were fully clothed, dressed in filthy blue jeans and baggy t-shirts with no outward sign of burns. Two of them were thin, short, and sported beards. The third one was much bigger than the others. He had long hair, wore a baseball cap, and sweatshirt. From across the street, I couldn't tell if they were missing teeth or if their teeth were black.

My chest burned from the heat of their presence. This look-feel was different from before. I asked KK, "Do you feel them?" She nodded yes. If we had let them see us, they might have caught and hurt us. These were desperate and different times. We had to be very careful in our approach. If they weren't nice, the cafeteria freezer would shelter us. I let KK know my plan.

We crawled over to the shop just before the cafeteria. It was kitty-corner to the supermarket. KK stayed put so I could see if they were friend or foe.

I said, "If I don't make it, take care of Tim, and find the shelter by yourself." I moved away from KK so she wouldn't be in their sight as I approached. Once I reached the street, I crouched down low and walked to the supermarket. I stood up straight and yelled, "Hi there." The three men stopped in their tracks. They turned slowly towards me. I walked closer to meet them.

One of them asked, "Where did you come from?"

"I just got here." I could see a wily smile beneath the dirt and hair.

"Are you alone?"

"Yeah, sure." They paused and glanced up and down the street.

They were near the cash registers next to the remaining shopping carts.

I asked, "Have you anything to drink?"

The big one said, "Sure but not much." He had a glass water bottle. I reached out to take the bottle. He grabbed my arm and spun me around. I was no match for his size and quickness.

I yelled out, "You're hurting me!" The other two came

in closer.

One of them blurted out, "He's small but better than nothing."

I yelled, "What are you going to do?" They laughed. I froze in horror. I guessed these men had turned into cannibals to survive. They were planning to eat me. I knew where we had to go.

I enticed them, "If you let me go, I'll show you my food hut."

Surprised, the one with the bottle asked, "What food hut?"

This caught their attention.

"I've been hiding in town and I've collected a lot of food and drinks, including liquor and beer. If you let me loose, I'll take you to it."

The water guy let me loose.

He warned, "You'd better be telling the truth or we are going to make you die hard."

I said, "Follow me," and walked across the street and pointed down towards the freezer. I yelled out, "There, inside the freezer." Sliding down to the basement then jumping over fallen beams didn't slow them down. They were spewing out threats laced with obscenities. There were bundles of bad food in the freezer covered with soot and smoke. I hoped that would fool them for a short time. That's all I needed. With their frenzy, it wouldn't be hard to get them in the freezer. The tough part would be shutting and locking the door before they escaped. I felt warmth radiating from the freezer. KK was behind the freezer and she knew the plan. She must have realized I needed help. I went to the freezer and barely opened the door. I stepped in. They almost knocked each other over getting in. They were yelling, "Where's the booze?" As soon as the last fellow had stepped in, the door slammed shut. It was dark. We had taken them by surprise. The outside handle made a clicking sound. KK had done her part. I closed my eyes and passed through the wall. Just then, I felt a tug on my arm as if someone had wildly groped out into the darkness. It was too late. I was too far out. KK put a piece of metal through the handle to stop them from unlocking the door. We made a great team together. I was learning to depend on her. I didn't intend to let these guys loose. KK didn't either. They were cannibal killers.

This diversion had put us behind schedule. KK and I climbed to the street level. The cannibals were yelling and pounding the door. It was hot in there and nothing would get better.

The hardware store had many tools. We had to find two pry bars. We had been there before and it had solid footing. We knew from our last visit there would be a pile of metal tools. KK spotted crowbars sticking out from under a large beam. When KK stood on them, they wiggled. She slipped them out. We returned to Tim.

Tim asked, "What took so long?"

KK answered, "Tell you later." Picking up the bars, more food and water from the carts, we started back toward the hill.

After a quick-paced couple of hours, we were back. Our food supplies were untouched. Tim pushed the food aside. I took the bar and jammed it in the hole. KK took the other one and wedged it in the groove around the edge. She and Tim had their hands around the bar ready to push. I counted to three and yelled, "Push." The cover moved to the side. It had loosened. I used my bar to push it over more. I looked down. It had white walls. It had to be watertight because I saw no dust, mud, or water. Looking down we could see ladder rungs and a hatch with hinges.

CHAPTER ELEVEN

Tim moved over to the hole and climbed down first. It was easy for him to make it down. KK and I followed him in. It wasn't a good idea to leave the bars, food, and water above ground so someone could trace our path. We stowed all the food and water below after a couple trips. Before closing the top cover, I wanted to make sure it was safe place. We had to find a way in. If you pulled back from the hole, things became dark. Feeling around, KK found the hatch. It had a lever. I pushed up on it. It opened. I couldn't believe my eyes. When I opened the hatch, I detected no additional human presence.

Hurrying back towards the light from above, I climbed back up the rungs. I pulled the cover over as far as I could. KK was watching from below. She climbed up with the crowbar and placed it under the cover lip. Using as much leverage as possible, she slid it in place.

Tim and KK went through the hatch first. This was no ordinary hallway. Dark wood lined the wall. Small runner lights lined the floor with dimly lit emergency lights in the ceiling. The air smelled like a freshly built wooden home. In the dim light, I could still see polished surfaces. We had found safety. KK's father wasn't exaggerating when he said the shelter was like a country club.

KK mentioned, "My father may be in here."

I said as nice as possible, "I do not feel the presence of anyone."

Sadly, she agreed, "Yes, you are right, neither do I. We three are surely orphans."

It was fantastic. The hallway was wide, with portraits hanging every few feet, and crown molding. Double paneled wooden doors were thick and heavy.

Each room had a small brass sign to identify it. We looked for the kitchen. We found a large dining room that could hold a couple hundred people at one time. More dimly lit emergency lights in the ceiling provided enough light for us to see the full layout. There were four doors, two swung into the kitchen, and two swung out. We entered the kitchen where the freezers were humming. It was a huge room. I tried the light switches, but no lights came on. I turned on the stove burners. They did not light. Tim opened the freezer. All kinds of food filled the shelves. I grabbed three loaves of frozen bread and put them on the kitchen worktable to defrost. KK tried the faucet. Water came streaming out, but it never turned hot.

We found glasses and drank. It was wonderful just having plain water. KK found a pantry with canned peaches, pears, apples, and much more. Tim and I scampered around looking for a can opener. Finally, Tim remembered the Swiss Army Knife. He used it to open the cans. He gave the first one to KK. Tim kept the next one and passed the knife to me. I opened a can of peaches. I felt sick after eating the entire can. We opened three more cans. KK and I finished a second one but Tim didn't. We sat on the floor, bloated up with fruit, syrup, and water while softly moaning how good it was. Our shrunken stomachs were too full.

KK commented, "There is so much food."

We were filthy from the mudflows, ashes, soot, and smoke, with bloody scabs from the scratches, bites, and cuts caused by the prickly world above. We found a big shower room. It said "Men" on the door. Inside the room, we found a cabinet with bars of soap, hand towels, and bath towels.

I told KK, "We're going to take a shower."

"Fine," she said, "I'll find the women's shower room." Off she went.

We went in, stripped, threw our clothes in a wastebasket, and took cold showers. The cold fresh clean water made us feel human again. I drank so much my stomach was sticking out.

Tim had playfully jumped in and out to get used to it. He had a lot of little boy left in him. The cold water had taken few minutes to get used to, but soon I was scrubbing down my cruddy skin. My dog and rat bites had dried up, but the soap was making them burn. I hurt all over and the cold water made my muscles tight.

The soot had passed right through our clothes so underneath we were entirely black. Tim was scrubbing hard with the towel and soap. I washed his filthy back. We then switched around. I turned my water off and grabbed a towel to dry off. Outside the shower room, we found light summer robes. Tim picked out the smallest one. Mine was too big. I rolled my sleeves up, the bottom still brushed the floor. There were stalls with toilets nearby with real toilet paper. This was luxury living. Struggling survivors like us forget about basic things like toilet paper and soap.

Before, the stooping position had been an unsafe posture, leaving us vulnerable to attack. We had used anything to wipe when we could. I went over to a stall and grabbed toilet paper to blow my nose. It felt so soft. We walked down the hallway and found the women's shower room. We sat outside waiting for KK to finish.

After KK finished her shower and joined us I said, "It's time to rest." We looked for sleeping quarters. Not too far from the showers, we discovered a large room with a king sized bed. At that moment, we were standing in front of a soft king size bed with a lavender-colored spread. It was as if we had gone back in time before doom-night, except this was our new family living together. Raising the sheets up, KK slid in. Tim jumped in right after her. I followed. We talked about exploring the complex in the morning, and one-by-one fell asleep. The morning would come soon enough. Exploring would be fun. My dreams were about the great things we'd find including ice cream, candy, and games.

It had been difficult to stay sleeping. This comfort was so abnormal. When I woke up, Tim and KK weren't there. I could hear Tim yelling in the hallway creating echoes. I found KK in the kitchen. Like me, she was still wearing her robe. Her half head of long hair was hanging down along one side of her body. Her burns and mine were at the point of scarring. Oddly, we were healing up amazingly fast, with no infection. We didn't recognize it as remarkable.

The hallways had small lights, but other rooms were dark. The kitchen had green lights on the freezer doors. KK dug out food from the freezer. She found a microwave oven, but it didn't work. I plugged it into the same set of sockets as the freezers. She defrosted food then cooked breakfast. The bread had defrosted. It was white bread, not my favorite bread. She had found powdered food supplies and mixed up milk with cold water and ice from the freezer. It was unbelievable. In the dining room, I arranged place settings for three.

Tim entered the kitchen. He had smelled the food. KK was carrying the last tray into the dining room. She invited us to sit. Tim pushed the kitchen doors against the walls so they would stay open. I pulled a table close to the doors. The bread was dry, milk was weak but cold, and sausages had cold spots. Tim like me scooped up food until it was all gone. KK helped herself to large portions too. She looked happy and proud to have fixed our first banquet.

She asked, "Did you guys like it?"

I grabbed my stomach and replied, "Are you kidding?"

We left dishes on the table.

Tim listed places he'd found. He had explored quite a lot. That included the game room with pool tables and a big TV, the gym with a small swimming pool, and staff quarters. He described the garden as a large room with bright lights over the plants. I asked if he'd seen an electrical room, he looked at me puzzled. I asked whether he had seen a room with a bunch of wires and switches. He shrugged his shoulders.

There were wall units by the doors with buttons. KK said they were probably intercoms. She suggested a government site would have a command center. If we found it, we'd have the plans for this place and our guessing game would be over. KK asked us to find a computer room. She suggested it would be close to the command center. She told us, "I attended special computer classes offered to dependents of service members. I am sure they would have a computer room here."

We had a lot more to discover. KK had turned into a real partner. Tim was still acting immaturely. He sat and listened to us and didn't seem to care as long as he had food and was safe.

Our jaunt found us first at the library. The library was like none I'd ever seen. There were fifteen tall blue colored units marked with Dewey decimals and categories of books. On the front of each unit computer screens with red and green buttons used to run the system. It was an automated retrieval system built for browsing. One unit labeled videos and DVDs caught my attention. When the electricity comes on, it would be worth a revisit. We returned to the hall. We still hadn't found a formal entrance.

The next door labeled "Club" was a lounge. KK

surmised, "If the club was here, the entrance will be nearby." She was right. The next door led to the "Reception". It looked like a hotel lobby with a set of couches, a few coffee tables, and a counter with computers on it. In an adjoining office, we found a desk with a phone and comfortable looking chairs. Tim picked up the phone receiver and said, "Hello." No one answered. He acted surprised.

On the counter was a stack of brochures. KK grabbed one and said, "These are exactly what we need." They pictured the entire site including floor plans. We located the utility room. The brochure mentioned the complex sat on twenty acres. We had found no other floors. It mentioned many space-saving concepts incorporated into the facility for both private living quarters and community areas to wander, play, and learn. The builders had spared no expense. It had the best of everything.

The pamphlet had something else, its name. It read, "Welcome to Home Fort Twelve," so we decided to call ourselves, "The Twelves."

I was sure there were other things to explore, but we needed to turn the power on. With Tim leading the way, we went towards the utility room. It was a straight shot down the hall. The designers had avoided creating a rat's maze in the main thoroughfares. We passed the dining room, kitchen, and staff quarters where we'd been before. We skipped a hallway before the staff quarters. According to the map, it was on the way to the gym and game rooms. When we got to the staff quarters, we found stairs leading to the basement. The utility room was under the staff quarters. The cabinets were gray with big handled switches. They each had serial numbers with a label. I found the one labeled "Lights" and tried it, pulling down seemed to do nothing.

I told Tim to check the hallway. I asked, "Are there any big lights on?"

He answered, "None."

I pushed the handle back the opposite way to where I found it. KK found another cabinet that read "Main" on it. She pulled the handle down and then I pulled mine. The lights came on! We were not used to the brightly lit hallway. KK pulled another handle labeled "Library." Each major area had its own switch box. This meant we could leave things off. I wanted to see and experience everything so I had KK pull them all. As power moved to the different rooms, we heard a small hum. Starting up of so many things at once produced a burning wire smell. Everything had power. We didn't touch the boxes already on. They had to be supporting power to the freezers, small nightlights, and other things continuously running.

Tim tired of exploring, so he headed for the game room. KK and I kept going. She led the way up the stairs to the second floor. We arrived at the guest quarters. KK said, "They look like luxury cabins on a ship. They copied the floor plan from a cruise ship and made similar rooms." Some guest rooms had one double bed while others had up to four bunk beds. Each had a desk, TV with large in-wall screen, DVD player, entertainment center, computer, bookcase, two or three chairs, and small lounge. Each desk had a small vase with silk flowers.

The hallway had two large restrooms for men and women. At one end, a linen exchange room led to a laundry room with large washers and dryers. The closed off room shielded guest quarters from noise and heat.

This quiet place gave me an eerie feeling because I expected to see people moving around and there were none.

I asked, "Do you feel queasy?"

"What do you mean?"

"It feels as if everyone has mysteriously disappeared and I might be the next to slip out of existence."

She looked me straight in the eyes, gave me a hint of a smile, and said, "Well, that is close to the truth, isn't it?"

This answer amused and bothered me. On the one

hand, my feelings were right on, on the other, KK's exceptionally insightful answer made me feel threatened. Until that moment, I had been the strong one with the answers, leadership, and let's not forget power. KK had made a subtle move. I had a choice to make. Should I be confrontational or hug her? I swallowed hard and took it as something good. Until then, we had been working well together. If she hadn't remembered Home Fort Twelve, we would still be out in the world avoiding other humans who were slowly turning into desperate mindless animals.

KK and I had to complete our exploring. The last floor was labeled "Security". We found the stairs leading to the third floor. This area was a lot different. It was more like an office building. Each room had a sign hanging high on the door. Military staff had manned this floor. The command center consisted of a communication room, watch room, small jail, and a small break room supplied with coffee makers, refrigerators, and kitchen supplies. At one end, there was a room with steel vault-like doors labeled, "Bomb Shelter." Next to it, an airplane styled lavatory.

We entered the watch room. What a big surprise. Large flat-screen computer monitors with date and time displayed on the bottom covered the walls along with a picture of each room in the facility. The control had buttons to scan rooms, switch a screen to another room, or zoom. KK and I, both, caught something moving on a screen. It was Tim in the game room playing a video game.

This was a sophisticated security system, yet it was easy to use. KK switched a screen to another room and back. The screen had the name of a view on the bottom and changed as she changed views. She switched to, "Garden." We both stood and stared at bushes, vines, and other plants. After being in the green-less world above, this was a real pleasure to see.

Alongside each switch, a button labeled, "Sound." I

pushed one for the game room. We heard video games as if we were in the room. None of this should have been a surprise since we were in a government created facility meant to secure the most powerful people in our country.

Four screens were off. KK went to the panel and found the corresponding numbers. She flipped the switch on the first one. It took us aback. In front of us was a real time satellite picture of Earth. KK sat down in the chair and fidgeted with a zoom button. We were astonished, as the picture got closer and closer to the Earth. We could see the hazy masses of clouds floating through the sky. As we got closer, it changed to display the zoom level. The bottom read in bold letters 20,000 miles, Earth. Zooming in more, it changed to 10,000, United States. Finally, it read Illinois. We looked at the picture, trying to pick out landmarks like the Mississippi River. KK scanned to find it but had no luck. The Mississippi river was gone. She zoomed in closer until it read Chicago. We saw no buildings or lakes. Chicago and the Great Lakes were no longer there. This was freaky. KK kept scanning to find our town. She found it. The screen said Bennington. She zoomed in to see the area where we had escaped the cannibals. The fire was still burning. We had seen enough. It was upsetting. Chicago, the Great Lakes, and Mississippi River were missing. An enormous threat had wiped out our world just as I feared. Alone, we had to take care of ourselves.

CHAPTER TWELVE

We were ready to leave the command center. I had to forget the communication or watch rooms for a short time. We had food, electricity, and lots of fun stuff right in front of us. We didn't need to face our situation, right then. I suggested, "Let's have fun." I pointed to Tim enjoying himself in the game room. I said, "Let's go see what he's doing." KK didn't hesitate. We ran up the stairs and found Tim lost in a video world. KK and I found games we liked. The big difference was there was no interaction between us. We found an escape from sorrow, fear, and heartbreak. Hours passed by. KK came over, hit me on the shoulder, and asked, "Are you hungry?" I left my game and went to Tim. He was asleep on a chair. I guessed his earlier excursions had caught up with him. I shook him, and I let him know, "Time to eat. Let's go." He followed along.

In the kitchen, I grabbed a few sausages and bread from the freezer and threw it in the microwave to defrost, then fried the sausages. Tim carried the sausages into the dining room. KK buttered our bread. I opened a storage locker that held cases and cases of soda and filled up a refrigerator.

I asked, "Does anyone want a drink?"

They both said, "Coke." I put ice in glasses and served cokes to them. It was another tasty meal. Leaving our plates as we did before was fine for us. We had no worrisome rodent or insect problems. Eventually, we'd have to clean. We went back to the game room and stayed there until it was time for bed. We returned to our room, crawled in, and covered up.

The pamphlet floor plan identified our chosen room as the commander's quarters. That explained the room size, extra furniture, and enhanced computer system. The only live greenery outside the garden was a small tree in his room. The rooms mimicked the commander's room with bright colors and an option to turn on simulated sunlight.

Another night had passed and we, The Twelves, were living high. KK and I both knew we had unfinished business on the third floor. We had to know what the world was doing.

After finishing breakfast and the requisite pit stop, Tim returned to the game room. He knew nothing about the communication room nor the intriguing watch room. We didn't think he cared. KK and I returned to the computers. She turned on all the screens. There were many screens and switches. We saw the northern and southern hemispheres. Earth's dark side was visible. The screen for those had a small red light with the words ultra-infra-red. We hadn't noticed that the previous day. No matter where we scanned the cameras, the results were the same. The Earth we once knew had irrevocably changed. It was as if someone had splattered the surface with big gobs of mud. The gobs filled the rivers and valleys. We tried to find signs of life in different places. It was like looking for planets in space. We zoomed out then zoomed in to find humans. At the lowest level of zoom, we could sometimes see something moving, but we couldn't get to the level of truly identifying them as people, animals, or vehicles. We were happy to see life scattered all around. KK was adept at using the equipment. All the while, we kept an eye on Tim.

We moved into the communication room. It had four phones and four computers. Beside each computer was a list of things to do to sign in, including a password. KK turned on a computer and attempted the sign in process. The first time she mistyped. She had to try again. As soon as she logged in, a notification popped up on the screen. It read, "You have mail." She opened the mail and selected the most recent notification. It turned out to be an error notice from the central computer telling us it had suffered a fatal error and it was in recovery mode. It said, "Please be patient." This notification seemed funny to us. Being patient for the system in a world that had been whipped into mush was so out of place. KK opened the next email that was three days earlier than the first one. It was from Home Fort Three to twenty other forts asking if anyone else had signed on. They wanted to know if anyone else had made it to a shelter. KK clicked the reply button and typed, "Yes, we are at Home Fort Twelve." She did not tell them our names or headcount. We had to be careful. I was glad KK was there to manage the technical stuff. She continued her perusal. Home Fort Ten reported they had six people at their location and the electrical systems had problems. One other fort had answered. It was Home Fort Nineteen. They reported two people there. The other emails were more system warnings. KK replied to Home Fort Ten. Maybe someone could tell us what had happened to our world.

We waited and waited but didn't get a response. KK opened another program to see what it contained. Someone was posting to a live news service on a government blog site. One posting described their situation. It said they were in a mountain sanctuary meant for the President. As far as they knew, the catastrophe killed the US officials and they were the only ones to survive. They had more than 100 soldiers and scientists there. Supplies weren't a problem. They hadn't posted an email address. We had no way to reply. They gave exact directions to their site just in case anyone needed shelter and could get there.

Another posting stated that a meteor or an alien weapon had struck Earth. Whatever the cause, the result was an estimate that over ninety percent of the world's population perished. Natural hazards, disease, and starvation would soon kill more. Scientists predicted that some insects and amphibian forms of life would survive fairly well, but the larger animals hadn't much chance to make it through. This was bad news, but not unexpected. Especially after what we had just viewed on our satellite scans of Earth. This was a new beginning for humankind. The world hadn't been so sparsely populated since prehistoric times.

There were quite a few posts from the mountain site. They were trying to reach out and help anyone they could. As we finished reading the posts, our screen beeped with the notification, "You have mail." I got excited. KK clicked on the mail from Home Fort Ten. They had replied exclusively to us. Their plight had worsened. Their freezers were failing. They were trying to run new power lines to them. If they lost the freezers, they would have to live on the canned and dried goods in the storage lockers. They knew that government had planned for two years and 200 people; their survival did not depend on freezers.

They were worried about people on the outside. They mentioned the continuous pounding on the front entrance. They had locked up the escape hatches and installed the front door reinforcement panel. To prepare for an intrusion, they had moved supplies into their bomb shelter. They had also shut off access to floors by locking doors between them. They sealed it up like a submerged submarine. They did not know how many were outside. They couldn't risk opening the fort up to possibly hundreds more.

They explained, "We are auditors with the guard, caught at the site during the explosion." The auditors knew all the tricks to keep safe. An audit included the validation that security devices worked. We learned a lot from their mail. There were four women and two men in their group. One woman was the guard escorting them. The others were auditors, all skilled engineers with years of practical experience. They mentioned that the third floor command center was the most secure. They also mentioned stored weapons. We had found no weapons. We hadn't done a comprehensive search because we'd spent so much time in the watch and communications rooms.

KK replied by telling them our ages. She said, "We have no system problems as far as we know," and explained how we found the fort. She mentioned blog postings from the mountain group and asked how many home forts existed. Home Fort Ten replied that there had been 102, eighty in the US and others in foreign countries for Americans and friendly officials. They said if we looked through the commander's room, we'd find the details of other forts, including locations and fort design. We learned that forts were close to being identical with a few differences due to environmental and topography considerations. They explained that teams of government contracted experts advised on design, supply, and ergonomics. This included a pilot program that had kept 200 people under surveillance in one site for more than a year to make sure forts could support numerous people.

They asked if she used the chat program. She didn't, but they explained how to open the chat window. KK followed their directions and hooked up in real time. After a half an hour, the person on the other end reported the pounding had ceased. They didn't know what it meant. When ten minutes had passed, the chatters interrupted with these words: "Explosion at front must go!" The connection went dead.

Neither KK nor I had noticed Tim's arrival. He had slipped in without a sound. Our look-feel had adapted to his presence. We were no longer in the watch room so we couldn't keep an eye on him.

He asked, "What are you doing?"

KK said, "We have email, a blog, and a chat exchange with Home Fort Ten."

He acted surprised when he heard they had been attacked.

He commented, "Lucky for us, our front door is covered up with mud."

Suddenly, I had a feeling other humans were present.

Our entry room wasn't locked from the inside and we hadn't fully put in place the safeguards mentioned by the auditors. Hurriedly, I took off to check the hatch. KK and Tim headed for the watch room. When I got to the hatch, someone had opened the top one and the second one just like us. This meant at least one other person was in the complex. I didn't know if they were a threat like the invaders at Home Fort Ten. After replacing the top cover, I locked up the second hatch and slid the heavy reinforced plate in place just below the bottom one. If they made it by the hatch from the outside, they would still have to get through the thick plate and the reinforced metal panel.

Part II Strangers

CHAPTER THIRTEEN

This was our fourth planet to cultivate for the zirns. It had been over 2,000 years since we first entered space orbits around our planet of Hight. As with all species, we were curious. We also knew our small world wouldn't last forever with the growing population and requisite pollution. Our prophets drove the space race with predictions of famine, drought, and disease. We believed them. They represented the truths of our world. So, all our combined energies were on holding back the ravages they predicted. We knew we wouldn't prevent them, but at the very least, we could make the expected pain less severe.

The other three planets were much smaller. A planet required enough liquid and arable land to make it viable. I, Wollen, the Chief Agriculturist, had the joy of evaluating the results. It was my first real assignment after leaving the lab. This was what I had devoted my life to ever since I was ten. That is when the government chose me, with hundreds more, to join the Saviors of our species. My test scores were among the highest ever achieved. I excelled in math beyond anyone else. They gave me the designation of "Savior." The government rewarded my family with extra benefits, including larger rations of food. Our sage leaders knew if they kept the parents happy, we children would be happier. The parents were always around to encourage us to continue. If we didn't, then the perquisites would've gone away.

In the beginning, the schools had general but accelerated instruction. We gradually moved into more lab work. Our professors kept our imaginations entertained and challenged enough to promote discovery and invention. The upper level programs fell into two main areas of study: space engineering and planet cultivation. My math background made me a better candidate for the engineering. My overall abilities qualified me for both areas. Professors assigned me to our weakest field of research, planet cultivation. Personally, I did not believe it was the right choice, but I gladly accepted it because we were all racing to prevent more loss of life. Besides, there was no other way for me to go without making my family pay the price.

For me, the studies were easy and by the time I was fourteen, I was in charge of my own project. Our task was two-fold. First thing was to create a process that would turn any fertile planet into a food source. Second, we were to develop new plants that would grow quickly, be low maintenance, and supply balanced nutrition. They broke us into different project teams going off in different directions. A worldwide system recorded our work. All others could share and search our results. The professors and leaders of a project took any new development and made it world news. Part of their job was to keep the common people of our world hopeful. They had control of all mass communication.

By the time I was fifteen, my project developed an idea for a plant that would be part vegetable and part animal. This approach was different from the other research paths. It was so radically different that we had to get special permission to pursue it from the Council of Saviors.

The Council had founded the program. Some Council members were politicians, but most were serious elderly scholars. I had no experience with them. They gave me an outline for the presentation and I put it together with the help of my team.

We traveled to the Council's headquarters, which included overnight stays for presenters. It took four hours to explain our idea. We answered mostly technical questions. The scholarly questions provided me with more ideas. I relied on my team members to answer the politicians. For me, it was too frustrating trying to translate their words into a real question. We left the chambers with no idea how they felt. Reading emotions from their demeanor was impossible. After a rough night of sleep, they called my name via the intercom system. I pushed the button to let them know I was awake. It was a public relations officer telling me we had approval and we could return to our labs. As soon as the approval came through, the public relations crew announced the plan to everyone on the planet. This was before we made it back home.

Soya Zirn was the first person to suggest an animal-plant combination. We had to let everyone know what the new animal would be called and decided on "zirns" in her honor. She was flattered. The public wasn't so kind because joining of two complete different systems such as plants and animals, seemed extreme. The underground-press labeled us crazy zirnians. Soya's family could hardly go out in public due to the hazing. The critics stared at our families and referred to us as a band of lunatics. This was coming from the conservative scientists and the fringe believers in the inevitable death of our planet. Our peers on the other project teams teased us. We would often see signs of sarcasm when they posted their current experiments and research. No matter, we had approval to go on. More importantly, we had a committed team to take the idea as far as we could. Our families were still receiving government extras. They didn't need to worry about persecution from a financial position.

After going through the red tape for approval, we had to add to our team. We, the original ten, didn't have enough background on animals. We selected five more people to join us. They committed to the new approach without reserve. At their insistence, we kept their appointment to the team secret.

During the first meetings, it was difficult getting along with one another. We kept coming back to the unifying idea of being the real Saviors of our people. Unified Saviors theme eliminated the petty bickering that existed among strangers.

I transferred an original team member who couldn't change. She ended up resigning from the program and her family lost their benefits. Everyone knew the unstated rule that if you wash out for any reason; the Saviors expelled you and you couldn't reapply. I was saddened that she had to leave, but the project came first. My understanding was that the Saviors had disbanded and expelled entire teams because of lack of performance or plausible solutions.

We broke into two groups, one to create the zirn animal-plant or what we called a planimal. The other group was dedicated to planet cultivation. I was the leader of both groups and provided the direction and integration necessary to make the split workable. I recruited an intern named Onard to be my Administrative Aide. The zirn team had eight members and the cultivation team had five, not counting me. Obviously, Soya was a zirn team member. We lived in the same complex where our work was being recorded by cameras and audio recordings.

We established methods for activity logging, change control, and reporting procedures. Team leaders assigned full time monitors to each of us.

Everything was in place. The government would fill any request, as fast as possible, with the help of a specially educated and connected supply team. Our world commercial and government institutions were already giving all teams carte blanche.

Other than our recent put-down via ridicule, the majority of Hight populace was behind us. This was a long-term commitment with no alternative because accepting the status quo meant the end of our civilization.

During the approval process, one unexpected piece of news had surprised me. As I was leaving the Council's quarters, I heard an announcement directing me to the message center. Once there, I found a folder. In the folder were the usual requirements regarding full disclosure, publicity rights, reporting processes, and documentation specifics. After that, a document marked secret had an entire section on the planet life expectancy. It involved all the studies on food, air, and water. There were projections on where the first mass deaths would occur from disease and starvation. There were comments outlining failed attempts to cultivate planets by other teams. The last warning at the end, stated, projects such as ours could be terminated without explanation and warning.

The second section had the most recent predictions from our prophets. They spoke of miscalculations on longevity and foretold of catastrophes soon to affect all scientific projections. This was the first time I had seen this information. The Council had changed the policy enough to let us working Saviors in on the truth.

The document's last section affected us the most. They demanded progress within certain periods or our project would be cancelled. The summation in the document explained that after studying our proposal, as wild as it was, they believed it could work.

They disclosed estimations of reaching our point of inevitable demise had changed to one year. Our downfall would be irreversible in one year. That was why they were only giving us nine months to finish. They apologized for the special requirement. As they explained, desperation drove their new policies.

I read the last section to the others on our presentation team. They became agitated and a look of hopelessness fell upon them. There were two concerns. The first was the unreasonable time to create a means to save the planet. The second concern was that if we failed in this short time, the perils existing in our world would destroy it a few months afterwards. We were panic struck. We had been comfortable believing we had years before the end. Our eyes were opened to the truth; truth that only we could change. After a short discussion of whether we could do it, we resolved it to be a moot question. Our minds had to focus on whatever it would take.

Thereafter, other teams submitted proposals. Some were having their project terminated without an explanation. A special bulletin notified others about the shortened deadline.

The space vehicle projects were creating more and more craft to support a plan to send many Hightians into space. The Saviors gave the project people, including those expelled reserved places on a spacecraft ready to speed away. Our leaders wanted to ensure the smartest of our civilization survived. Other projects would have their buildings, dirt, air, waste, zoos and plants stripped of any nutrients that might save Hightians while tearing down and killing all other things. These short-term solutions would last long enough for other last-ditch efforts to come into play. There were rumors about a subversive organization planning wholesale cannibalism. Some suggested the government had already built the facilities necessary to keep the chosen ones alive through cannibalism or genocide. Most of us didn't take these rumors seriously.

When we arrived at the lab, I called a meeting with everyone and confirmed the project approval. I also let them each have the secret documents with the nine-month due date. They were stunned, but all said the same thing, "We must start now, today!" They joined in with a vow to work nonstop until we, the real Saviors, finished the job.

Until that moment, I had my doubts about carrying on. When I felt the spirit they had, it was enough for me to believe we could do it. The teams started work the next hour. I followed the planned meeting times, giving relief for experiments that couldn't be abandoned just for the sake of a status meeting. Semantic jousting took place during those early periods. Eventually, we developed into expert teams working under unbelievable pressure.

The cultivation team was making notable progress from the beginning. They came up with the idea to use liquids from a planet to loosen layers of dirt and flatten hills and mountains. The idea was to introduce a liquid attracting agent into the atmosphere to capture all the water into clouds. After they reached a point of saturation, the water with the agent would rain down on the planet, foaming the soil up so it would ooze over everything. The wave of foamy mud would carry so much force it would crush everything in its path. After seven months we had, working models in the lab and were preparing for a test on a nearby small moon.

The zirnians had a bigger challenge. They started things off with a debate on whether they should use existing animals and plants and just change them. Others wanted to grow something in a test tube. They had created a wish list to begin the project. It included the nutritional needs, size, growth rate, delivery vehicle, planting process, planting limits, environmental requirements, harvesting plans, intelligence, and possible training requirements. The last two items were important in the decision to use an animal that already existed. They determined it would take too long to create a new animal and ensure it had the required intelligence.

This plantimal would be a self-propagator like many plants with seeds. Unlike normal plants, it would need to be smart enough to recognize where to root itself and to relocate if needed. Ideally, the zirn would self-harvest when it reached maturity. Conceptually, instead of having an animal that ate vegetation to live, zirns would use the same food source as plants and bypass the need for eating and digestion. Another key was to control the instinctual signals and use them to find locations for self-planting and harvesting.

The zirn team had split up to work on various ideas. One group thought animals with fur or hair were the best candidates. Fur and hair would grow into edible products along with the body. The others wanted an altered root to feed the animal directly and be a source of food. The team stayed split for two months. We had at our disposal hundreds of years of genetic research and DNA alteration knowledge. To provide as much food as possible we had learned to speed up the growth cycle on plants and animals. That was exactly the knowledge we had spent so many years in school learning.

After much experimentation, the root team gave up and joined the other team. They couldn't figure out how the zirn could extricate itself from a long or bulbous root. Their work didn't go for nothing. They had learned how to combine the life support system of an animal into a root system. They planned for the root to stay in the ground after harvest. The zirn would self-harvest after producing adequate cover and body.

We tested three animals in eight months. The most favored was the freme. It was a small animal with heavy fur, four legs, and a pleasant disposition. Every passing day proved to show the freme's genetic makeup lent itself to our solution. The team had altered its DNA, joined it with plant growth, and reproductive instructions. Their procreation no longer depended upon animal intercourse but on root propagation. The root system fed the fur directly. It was a multi-plant vegetable garden. One harvested ripe animal could feed one person for two weeks. The animal nourished itself through a newly developed stomach that received nutrients via the fur grown into the ground. It also used the small amounts of exotic gasses in the atmosphere. Energy needs were low for the stationary creature because it lay dormant. The small amount of waste it produced fertilized the ground. The plan was to drop the animals as small pellets to the surface. They would find a planting site, grow to maturity, and then sit dormant until harvest. Maturity would only take four months.

The planet cultivation team had been working with the space engineers to provide the craft and systems to create a shipping environment for the zirns.

The project team tested on three different moons in our solar system. I attended the comprehensive acceptance test. It was outstanding. After we released the liquid attraction agent, we positioned ourselves just above the atmosphere. We could see the lakes and rivers dissipating as they became smaller and smaller. Heat from the chemical reaction caused plumes of steam. The resultant clouds grew larger and darker as time passed, causing highly charged air, and lightning. Just as predicted, the water mixed with the foaming agent and fell to the surface. The foaming agent slowly changed the colors and shapes below as if a magic wand waved over the moon. The results weren't conclusive because the moons were small and without strong gravity. Based upon computer models, we could predict success on larger targets. The entire team attended the technical readiness review. They had already scouted in space for the first four planets to cultivate. They considered the atmosphere, soil volume, liquid types and volume, planet size, topography, and present vegetation. All four planets met the zirn needs. The team reported the results from the moon experiments, planet scouting, and models to the Council. Public relations spun the results out to the entire planet.

Onard made sure our progress reports were always on time. They hadn't shut us off. After eight and a half months, we had one problem left to solve. The team didn't believe they could solve it in two weeks. I asked for a special session with the Council of Saviors to provide status, show our progress, and to request at least two more weeks. If I waited for the last day, it would be over before I had a chance to say anything. I arranged for the trip to the Council.

The agenda listed me, Wollen, as the Project Leader and Soya as Chief Scientist. My presentation on the zirns was brief. I knew it was one thing to read progress reports and news report verses seeing the real thing. I needed to get as real as possible. Soya accompanied me. She would be the ultimate planet Savior. After a brief introduction, Soya came to the podium. The podium stood higher than the Council did, letting her speak down to them and they had to look up at her. She had a deep voice and carried a basket covered with a towel. Presenting the reports on craft readiness, on planet selections, and zirn status raised her prestige level with the Saviors. The most senior scientist stood up and interrupted. He asked, "What do you have in the basket?" She paused for a second and then raised the basket. She pulled the towel off to find a zirn, fully developed. It was a beautiful sight.

The entire Council stood. I reached behind and grabbed more covered baskets and waved to the standing attendants to come and pick up baskets filled with zirns. They gave one to each Council member. I stood next to Soya to support her. She told the Council they were looking at the future of our world. The Council didn't know what they had. Soya explained our workable plan to create gardens beyond our wildest dreams. She said our team had finished an impossible task in less than nine months. Council members were speechless. They focused on Soya with startled expressions of dismay. They were realizing we had come with the only thing that might save our species. We could see their crevice filled grim faces turn into beams of hope.

I relieved Soya and told them I had one issue remaining. I said, "As you know, we want these animals to self-harvest based upon their instinctual controls." They all nodded in agreement. I pleaded, "This is the remaining issue, and we need a two-week extension." They were not accustomed to theatrics. A politician stood up and suggested adjournment. It was a natural move for him when he faced decisions. The Council adjourned. The next morning, they sent a message to Soya and me. They approved our extension. Giving us two more weeks was not too risky when in less than four months the planet would be doomed.

Self-harvesting had to allow for changing soil and variable weather, regrowth, terrain, and the harvesting of zirns. We had to make our crops as self-sufficient as possible. The design was to have the zirns wake from their dormant existence at certain stages of maturity. They would then determine in less than a month's time if regrowth was possible in their location. If conditions were poor, they would have to leave their current location and migrate to another area. They would become like other animals instinctually moving to better food and watering locations except they would recognize levels of fertility. When they matured fully, their root system would stay planted and the animal part would move to collection sites. Once we determined how to attract the zirns to the collection sites, the rest was, accomplishable based on our proven ability to train animals and alter instinctual behavior. One issue we couldn't overcome was rough terrain. We didn't have time to tackle this problem. I personally deemed it the least important in the beginning. I made this decision even though I knew that the smaller problems ignored in the beginning would eventually become the most important.

That drama led up to our last presentation. Our team had made the deadline. It had been four months since the first nine-and-a-half-month period. On Hight, we had seismic activity, floods, and high winds. The lack of land with increased demand made our agricultural system inadequate. Reports from the other sites proved our planting went well. We had close to seventy-five percent zirn coverage. Our first harvest started and the people of Hight had the beginnings of a plentiful food supply.

CHAPTER FOURTEEN

I didn't join Tim and KK in the watch room because I wanted to confront the intruder. The watch room was an advantage for us and besides, we were acquainted with the complex. I went to the intercom box.

I asked, "Can you hear me?"

Tim answered back, "Where are you?"

"Stay where you are." The camera on the wall turned in my direction. I figured KK was on video surveillance. I waved at the camera and stayed by the intercom.

My heart was pounding hard while breathing short and fast. My mind was racing with the different ways to approach an intruder. I hoped they'd already left but then I realized that wouldn't be a good thing because they could return with more scavengers. I worried that there would be too many for us and we would become the victims. It was tough standing by the intercom waiting for KK to let me know what was going on.

Although it was only a few minutes, it was an eternity.

KK called and said, "Someone is in the kitchen."

I asked, "How many?"

She answered, "So far only one, a very thin pale looking man. He is talking to himself and ripping open loaves of bread."

I directed her, "Keep scanning for others in different rooms, but keep an eye on the kitchen."

I couldn't afford to make my move too early. KK took a few more minutes and finally reported that she saw nothing else. I went to the watch room to see for myself. By the time I got there, Tim had left. I asked, "Where's Tim?" She hadn't realized he was gone. My eyes caught motion from the surveillance screen aimed at the hallway leading to the kitchen. Tim had headed for the kitchen holding a crowbar. He wasn't following our motto to take it slow and be careful. I reminded KK, "Stay alert." I hurried down the hall towards the kitchen.

In the kitchen, the thin pale man had his hands around Tim's head. He was close to breaking his neck. When I entered, the man was facing the opposite way. He hadn't immediately noticed me. Tim's crowbar had fallen on the floor; I grabbed it, rushed towards the intruder, and swung as hard as I could at his head. The blow missed his head, but hit his shoulder. Tim fell limp to the floor with a thumping sound. The intruder turned and faced me. His face was twitching with a hateful look and eyes bulged out. He was making low growling sounds. I could smell his vomit-like body odor. KK yelled something through the intercom speakers, but the situation was too chaotic for me to understand.

I moved closer to the door preparing to escape and possibly distract him away from Tim. I swung the bar back and forth at his head. He ducked away from each swing. I hit him on the forearm, but it didn't seem to stop him. With one loud guttural growl, he grabbed the bar and pulled me next to him. He lost the bar, wrapped his arms around me, and lifted me off the ground. My arms were dangling behind him. He was trying to squeeze the life out of me. He shook me vigorously while raising me up and down. I could barely breathe. A tingling sensation flowed through my body, warning me that I was close to passing out. I bit him on his face. He let me fall. I grabbed the bar, stood up, and swung it towards his ear. The first blow went unnoticed. After two more strikes, blood was on the bar. The blows bloodied his face and his eye looked more popped out. He pushed me backwards knocking me hard to the floor again. The bar dropped out of my hand. He was standing almost on top of me. One hand was feeling around his battered head to ascertain damage. He let out a small yelp. This made him angrier and crazed. He looked down at me with his face riddled with pain. My blows had made him more of a hateful monster.

He looked so big standing above me. I was reaching for the bar when I felt his kick to my stomach. That kick knocked the rest of my breath out. I felt myself losing consciousness. I grabbed his leg, hoping to stop the next kick. He lifted it up and shook it. I slipped off. I expected the next kick to put me out for good.

He stopped in mid kick. His eyes looked as if he had been shocked. His face scrunched up with a look of pain and then surprise. A gasp came from his throat, a loud hiccup followed by the release of a long breath. His foot came down softly to the floor and he half-turned towards his backside. He didn't complete the turn before he fell on top of me. I felt his boney shoulder land on me. Then his head bounced on my face with a hard knock. I felt suffocated under him. I wasn't fully conscious.

KK had his legs and twisted one over the other to roll him off. As his back became visible, I saw a large knife sticking out from his upper back.

KK had realized we were in serious trouble after seeing Tim beaten.

After yelling on the intercom, "Hold on, I'll be there!" She hurried to the kitchen. The time between her yell and arrival seemed so long, but in reality, it was just minutes.

She told me, "I knew where the intruder was standing and he would've taken me out as soon as I entered through the door. I saw you fall as I slipped through the wall. I grabbed the knife and stabbed him."

When I was free, I just laid there. She went over to Tim. He was still unconscious. She took a cup of cold water and poured it over him. He rolled over, grabbing his arm. I sat up and slipped over to the wall for support. Tim was still flat out with KK trying to get his arm into a comfortable position. The intruder's corpse was just a few feet away. KK was in control. She went to a closet and brought back a blanket. She laid it next to Tim. We rolled him onto the blanket and pulled him to our bedroom. Together, we got him into bed. KK used a large soup spoon for a splint and wrapped Tim's arm.

She asked me, "Are you okay?"

"I am sore across the chest but nothing else hurts." KK suggested we take the intruder's body to the garden until we could get rid of it. We took the same blanket used for Tim and rolled the body onto it. We dragged him to the garden. I volunteered to dig a shallow hole. KK went back to nurse Tim. I dug the hole and pushed the body in. After packing it down, I joined KK and Tim in the bedroom. Even though Tim had acted foolishly, we had risen up to protect ourselves and had come out alive.

KK and I stared at each other. We were feeling a presence. This time it felt different from the other times. It felt close. I hurried to the watch room to start the scanning. KK stayed to rest and guard Tim.

CHAPTER FIFTEEN

This last planet was the largest one to be cultivated. We knew from the beginning that there were structures like mountains, hills, and canyons that might cause problems. We detected unnatural structures and attributed them to intelligent beings. Our urgent food situation and need for farming territory didn't allow physical visits to a planet. Our Hightians were much more important than any insignificant inhabitants. I must admit, there were a few historians, environmentalists, anthropologists, and archeologists who wanted to first study each planet. Our leaders decided early on that we had no resources to dedicate to such frivolous endeavors. I, Wollen the leader of expeditions, had spent the best years of my life dedicated to saving our planet. It was impossible to consider any further delays. No one on the project cared about what existed anywhere else or what the impact of our chemicals would be on inhabitants.

The Saviors had chartered us to bring in the crops. Our superior science and technological abilities ruled the universe without need of exploration. We already owned it all by default, with nothing to conquer.

Before planting zirns, we surveyed cultivation results.

These surveys were crucial and urgent. We knew we shouldn't take too much time after cultivation to send the zirns in to start their propagation. The success rate planting depended on how long we took. After they'd been through one growing cycle, it should not matter because of their self-sustaining nature as a mature plant.

The survey results were in and we determined the last planet had too many uncovered areas. The planet size or the structures may have caused the problem; we couldn't be sure from our ship. These areas would cause blight and reduce projected total output by interfering with the self-harvesting and replanting. Our project counted on every planet to supply enough food in time to save lives. We had no way to process another planet because resources weren't prepared. We had to send a crew to the planet surface for a cause and effect determination. Onard, Soya, and I were the only ones with enough knowledge for sufficient practical analysis and research.

We validated the test results from the last small moon. We knew what to look for and we could resolve problems. This was the first time since those tests that anyone had to leave our ship. Soya and I were prepared to do it again. We saw it as a challenge and possible way to improve the system. The first three planets went so well; our process had become routine. Those first planets becoming a mass of soil and the zirn planting was exhilarating. It was time for us to improve upon what we had done. This trek to one of our farms would raise interest and intrigue.

Our planet scanners detected life forms still in existence. We could essentially detect the movement of individuals. We couldn't tell what form they would take or if they were dangerous. The other sites had no inhabitants. In light of that discovery, we agreed to take two security guards with us.

The security guards had invisible shields that could envelope Soya and me in case of an attack. A voice command could turn on the shields from the ship. They acted like an anti-matter device. If something physical was threatening us, it would explode the object into sparks. If it was an energy force, it would absorb the energy.

Soya and I wouldn't have any personal weapons. We had to carry our analytical instruments to document conditions and take samples. Our eldest security people trained the guards. Their training included self-sacrifice for the protection of their wards. We were all wearing range-limited remote locator devices.

We took the shuttle down to the surface to visit multiple areas while investigating varied anomalies. The planet's atmosphere was compatible to ours. That made breathing devices and special clothing unnecessary. Our aim was to scout the perimeters of bare areas to determine why they were uncovered. The flight down was short though it took substantial time to find a safe landing place. It involved a lot of skipping around and hovering for the security check. After eight hops, we found a place classified yellow for security. Red meant we couldn't land. Blue meant we could land. Yellow meant that the landing place was okay, but living things were a possible risk. The shuttle landed in a low ravine surrounded by big boulders.

The guards left the shuttle. They went to the surface to test the air and to scan the surroundings while we disembarked. Our shuttle had scanners. They weren't good for far distances once we landed. They were automatically checking for life forms. Before Soya was to head down to the surface, a warning light came on signifying life nearby. We stayed inside and watched the guards walk towards the life forms. Our scanners showed life forms heading toward the guards. We could tell from our scanners that the life forms were separating. They were circling around our landing site. It was difficult to tell how many there was while they were moving. The guards must have known from their sensors that they were still moving towards them. The life forms stalked the guards. Soya was astounded that within minutes of landing, something had discovered them as prey. She asked, "How did they find them so fast?"

The boulders gave up their secrets. High above and encircling the guards were twenty striped creatures making loud roaring sounds. The guards had never seen creatures such as these. It was clear from the staring down and growling, the creatures meant them harm. The guards stood back-to-back waiting for an attack.

The creatures seemed angered and hostile. After the biggest one growled, two of them went down the side into a small ravine. They circled the guards. The guards clutched their small t-ray guns tightly while staying focused on the creatures.

They were treating the confrontation as a game. As they were watching the two, the leader quickly sent two more. The four were moving around trying to catch their attention. They paced back and forth. The guards didn't turn on the shield. The largest beasts rushed towards the guards. Both guards swung around and fired their weapons. Before the guards could turn the other way, another creature jumped them from behind. One guard fired the t-ray just as a striped monster landed on him. The leader sent down three more fighters. Another one jumped towards the guards and they both fired again, hitting the target. As the creature was splitting into invisible atoms from the hit, three large beasts from above pounced upon the guards. The beasts held down their arms with the guns and clawed them loose as others came in and ripped at their protective uniforms and into their flesh.

The guards had underestimated their quickness and tactics. They lost their lives in doing so. Soya and I watched the activity from the shuttle viewing port. The creatures tore their bodies apart and carried them away. The guards were lost. It looked as if we couldn't disembark at will.

Soya remarked, "This place deserves to be completely

cultivated." I immediately called the ship and let them know what we had witnessed. It was clear the guards had been negligent, causing their own demise.

I asked, "Can we get more security?"

They reminded me, "You have the only shuttle." We would have to rejoin them to get more security. Soya suggested we could out wait the creatures and then carry on with our work when they left. I said, "We'd have to pick a deadline." We had no choice. Our Hightians needed food.

CHAPTER SIXTEEN

After the episode with the intruder, we were saddened and appalled at having to kill a person. Handling the body would have been the last thing I wanted to do. The mixed feelings KK and I were sharing added to our discomfort. We were puzzled and leery.

I went to the watch room intending to discover the reason for our uneasiness. I dug around for manuals. One described how to put the cameras on auto scanning. The instructions were easy to follow. The system allowed all cameras to be on auto scan. I put two cameras on scanning. This way I would have two cameras moving around the rooms while the others stayed in one place. One camera was on KK and Tim. KK had fallen asleep next to Tim. Both looked peaceful and calm. I read that the cameras could be set up to detect motion and then point towards the motion automatically. I turned off the auto scanning and put the cameras on motion detection. The detection was set up to blink the screen when a camera found motion. The garden screen blinked immediately. It had artificial wind blowing on the plants so it would be a room with motion and thereby cause continuous blinking. Shortly afterwards, the kitchen screen blinked. The intruder came to mind, but he was dead and buried. I wondered whether someone else had broken in after him. I couldn't believe that was the case. Our guard was down. I needed KK and Tim back with me. Even though Tim was hurt and in shock and KK was emotionally drained, I couldn't risk having another intruder finding them. I switched the intercom on in the bedroom and called out for KK. She looked up at the cameras. I announced, "We have another visitor."

I fixed my eyes on the hall they would have to use to return while watching the kitchen. It looked all clear. Tim could hardly walk. KK had her arm around him almost dragging him. The kitchen screen blinked again. I saw something under the sink. The camera didn't swing fast enough to show it well. I wondered if an animal had somehow gotten in. What could be in that small space? KK and Tim joined me. I briefed them on the situation. Tim couldn't be any help this time. I explained the motion detection mode to KK. She understood right away. I suggested we wait things out together before we investigate. Tim laid on the floor moaning.

The screen flickered again. KK and I both saw it. It was a small arm swinging out of the cupboard. It was reaching down for scraps of bread dropped during the tussle with the last intruder. Our new sense was warning us there was an intruder, but this small arm wasn't the entire cause, only part of it. We let the motion detection scan continue. The hidden arm was the only thing moving. I went to the kitchen to confront whoever was there. KK said, "I'll watch your back." We let Tim sleep.

Arriving at the kitchen, I picked up Tim's bar. I used the bar to swing the door open. There in the cupboard was a small girl. She was in a dirty nightgown and she looked two or three years old. Mud covered her face. She seemed more like a clay garden statue than a real person. As I swung the door open, she shrugged with fright. KK was watching. I closed the door on the girl and checked each cupboard and freezer for anyone else. There were no others.

I called out for KK to come to the kitchen. She had to be the first one who related to the girl. Before KK arrived, I reopened the cupboard door. She was quiet and just stared up at me. I guessed the other intruder brought her in, or she had been following him to pick up scraps of food. KK entered the kitchen. She poured a glass of water and offered it to the girl. The girl hadn't spoken. She drank the water down vigorously. KK found crackers and brought them over for her. She stuffed them into her mouth. KK took her hand and gently pulled her to a standing position. She gave her another glass of water. KK asked, "What is your name?" No answer.

KK fed her sweet pears, and then she took her to the shower room. Afterwards, she led her to the commander's room where they crawled into our big bed. She fell asleep lying next to KK. I went to the command center. Tim was still sleeping. I woke him up and sent him to the bedroom. His legs seemed better after resting. It must have been the unnatural curative power we had acquired. The big soup spoon stuck out from the wrapping on his arm. I watched on the camera as he crawled gingerly up into the bed next to KK and fell asleep. He hadn't noticed our newest arrival.

I couldn't sleep so I stayed in the watch room. Scanning the map for other forts, I found the nearest was over 250 miles away. We could walk there if we ever had the need. It was Home Fort Fourteen. I saw no need and had no desire to venture out for a long time.

CHAPTER SEVENTEEN

Without guards, Soya and I had to be more cautious. No one was around to watch out for us. The striped furry creatures were the first to show. They were the hunters. Our guards had been foolish taking on those ferocious creatures. After the furry striped creatures, the howling clowns moved towards us. We didn't know if they were dangerous. Soya started a few motors on the shuttle to scare them. The vibration and noise frightened them off.

I found more t-ray guns in the arsenal. She and I weren't the best with these, but we had a short session in earlier training. Soya found a life detector scanner. We picked up a survival pack that included liquids, medicines, and food. We were unsure how long it would take to perform the survey. Our best guess was no less than a day but at most two.

We disembarked from the shuttle. We did a visual check on the shuttle to make sure the hatches were intact. I wasted no time and took the lead. The creatures were making sounds around us. Soya suggested we shoot anything that appeared to be alive. I agreed readily after watching the guards ripped into small pieces.

Our t-rays could last for a couple hundred shots. I

suggested we set them to a spraying stream so our lack of expert marksmanship wouldn't be an issue. The spraying stream was small at the nozzle but became broader as it moved towards a target. A wide spraying setting would reduce the number available shots.

Any one particle ray was enough to kill any size creature. The danger of hitting one of your own with the spraying stream stopped most soldiers from using it. Since there were only two of us, both novices, spraying wouldn't be as dangerous.

Buzzing winged creatures surrounded us soon after we left the shuttle. Understandably, we didn't know what to do. They were numerous. They filled the air all around us. We had no such things in our world. They landed on our exposed skin and sucked our body juice leaving a stinging sensation. We were down in a windless rock-surrounded ravine. We couldn't use our t-ray gun to blow away these tiny things. It was getting worse. We covered up as much as possible and moved quickly to avoid them. As we passed a small pond, the air filled with them and they sought us out. I was tempted to head back to the shuttle but I kept climbing higher. Soya was crying. These pests were making her angry. Finally, we were just under the rim. As we crossed over the rim, the wind swooped down upon us. The bugs went back below.

I questioned if what was happening was due to our recent cultivating or was it normally so uncivilized. It didn't matter but finding these varied creatures was important. We would need to take into consideration the impact on the zirns with this infestation.

It wasn't long before another encounter began. Soya noticed it first. She yelled, "Watch out!" It was gray and had a long protruding appendage from its head. It raised the appendage up and made a trumpeting sound. Soya moved quickly after I hit the ground. Her shot hit it in the head. The ray left nothing afterwards for us to see. It just faded out as each particle split then split again into nothing. It happened so fast that a blink of an eye would make you think it never took place. Shortly afterwards, we saw large black creatures hovered over the remains of another. These things had wings and a long red neck. Soya had her t-ray pointed at them. They were busy with the carcass and didn't notice our passing. It was better to let them live than to take chances with our spraying ray or an attack. All the creatures seemed dangerous.

Up to this point, we had encountered nothing that could be labeled intelligent. There were only these strange creatures with the strange sounds and smells. The terrain seemed to be random. We knew from our earlier pattern scans that some objects were more symmetrical. Moving through the tall green bushes and trees, we saw a red structure with multiple floors. This was something created by more intelligent beings than the ones we had come across. Soya kept a visual record via a recorder in her glasses. She also spoke into the microphone with notations from both of us. The recorder sent the data back to our ship orbiting the planet. Our peers on the ship could ask her to stop and get a fixed view of our newest discovery. Our ship relayed the information to Hight. On Hight, the Saviors were watching the entire operation. They had assembled special teams to perform analysis on what we found.

As the terrain, creatures, and commentary changed, the teams would contribute their questions, thoughts, and warnings to the system but not to us. We were data collectors. The request for stillness or the request to turn a certain direction would come to us. The Saviors sent one personal comment thanking us for our courage and reminded us how important this was to our world. Soya and I were ready to give our lives if need be.

We scanned the red structure. It picked up creatures. The count was not clear because the creatures were crowded together. We approached the structure with great caution. We discovered an entrance. Stepping inside, we stood still for a moment feeling out the structure. Bones were everywhere; the floor glistened with blood. We knew from the scanners the creatures were located higher than the first floor.

I imagined the Saviors and scientists frozen to their screens watching us. One part of me wished I was also on the outside with them.

Soya and I both heard a loud, frightening, and challenging growl. We'd heard the same sound during the attack on the guards. Looking up at the inside balconies on the second floor, we fixated on a room where creatures showed up on the scanners. The first one ran out and darted to the left. Soya fired. I shot the second one. Soya's eyes darted back to the door. Another leapt over the railing onto the first floor right in front of us. We both fired at it. On top, two entered. We raised our arms to fire when one from behind pounced on Soya's back. Soya's scanner flew towards the wall and splintered. The two from above leapt to the floor. I shot one while it was in the air. The other moved towards me and I shot it. I turned towards Soya. She wasn't moving a muscle. I was still upright, so I became the primary target. One turned towards me.

CHAPTER EIGHTEEN

I fell asleep in the watch room. Tim was the first to wake up in the bedroom. He shrieked when he saw the little girl's legs. It was enough to wake up everyone. My monitors were blinking with his movement. KK sat up to see what was wrong. The frightened girl rolled over and cried.

Tim shouted loudly, "Who is that?" KK explained how we had found her in the kitchen.

Tim asked, "Why didn't you wake me?"

"You have to rest to recover." KK turned her attention to the girl. At least her crying meant she could make sounds. Her lack of speech might be due to something other than a physical condition. I let them know I was coming down to be with them for our first breakfast with the newest family member. They went to the bathroom to freshen up. I made my way to the kitchen.

By the time they were finished in the bathroom and showers, I had eggs frying and toast buttered. Tim showed up first. He carried the toast into the big dining room. I fixed a bowl of quick rice in the microwave. The place smelled like our downtown cafe on Sunday mornings. KK and the girl arrived after the rice was cooked. I carried the food in. Tim fixed his toast. He had it layered with butter and jam. The girl clutched a piece of toast. I looked at her and asked, "What is your name?" She did not reply. We couldn't keep calling her little girl. We had to give her a name. KK suggested, "Name her Eleanor, the same as my mother." Tim surprised us with his suggestion of Maria. He wanted to name her after the server we lost at Bishop's. KK and I agreed that was a good choice. Maria, the clean and well fed little girl had dark circles around her eyes. She had lost everything as we had, but I'm sure it was harder for her to understand.

We went to the game room. Tim turned on the music. He knew exactly what he wanted to hear. KK set up the pool table so she and Tim could play. Maria and I sat against the wall watching them knock the balls around with not much success. Tim started to play pinball. His sore arm with the impromptu splint did not make it easy.

Maria was still not interacting with us. She stood close to Tim's machine, staring at the different colors. As Tim slapped his machine, Maria giggled. She slapped the side too. It looked as though she was coming out of shock. We played other games together and for a short time, it seemed we were just kids playing at the arcade. Suddenly KK stopped playing her game and turned towards me. I felt her staring at my back. Neither of us said anything. I instructed Tim to take Maria to the television lounge where he and Maria could stay occupied.

KK and I went to the command center. We had unfinished business to take care of. We both knew that something strange was happening around us. It was our look-feel. It had picked up something. We felt the presence together. It wasn't the same as when we felt the humans in our fort. The watch room was our only connection to the outside world. It would take two of us to understand all the complex dials.

In the computer room, KK opened email. She copied

the list of forts and pasted them into the send-to list. She started it with "Attention all other forts – please respond to establish contact." It didn't take long. Home Fort Nineteen and Three replied. Home Fort Ten was silent. No one else answered. KK asked if anyone had any more information. Home Fort Three replied that the presidential shelter had more postings. They informed us that the consensus among all, was that aliens had attacked our planet. Home Fort Nineteen reported spotting new and unusual orbit activity via their satellite monitor. We needed to know more. KK asked Nineteen to explain how they detected the orbit activity. They mentioned the online tutorial, provided specific notebook page numbers for important instructions, and finally details on how to operate space viewing. They mentioned the system could zero in on a specific location to a detailed level. We had already discovered how to zoom down towards Earth. We never thought of using it to watch our backs against aliens from space. KK asked if they heard from Home Fort Ten. A mob most likely destroyed it according to Fort Nineteen and Fort Three. No one mentioned contact from any other fort. Maybe they were not responding out of fear. They suggested it wouldn't be surprising if occupants didn't know how to work this email. KK let them know we had an intruder. After hours of email back and forth, KK and I had enough information to move on. She sent goodbyes from The Twelves. It felt wonderful being in contact with other humans even though there were so few.

We looked up the online tutorial and found out it detected aircraft. Next, we checked out the orbits. When we set the screen appropriately, it showed orbit paths by each sector of our hemisphere. In one sector, a blinking red path appeared. The other fort had picked up the new orbit and caused the display alert. Other orbit paths had objects shown in place. Designers of this system had planned well by including the view of space with the present-day orbits shown. It was easy for novices like us to pick out the anomalies. Something foreign was over Earth. We turned the viewer towards our location and zoomed down as far as we could, but nothing looked peculiar. We fixed the screen onto our location and turned on the motion detector. It couldn't distinguish between humans or animals.

CHAPTER NINETEEN

Soya was face down from the attack with her glasses splattered out in front of her. Her t-ray sat loosely in her hands. This time she couldn't come to my rescue. A vicious monster approached me. I moved to the side as it jumped towards my head. It scratched part of my face with its large claw. The blow to my head knocked me off balance. I fell on my back. My eyes blinked. I heard a thud behind me. Another beast had jumped towards me. It was the leader from before. He had been waiting for the right moment. I aimed the ray with both my hands just above my head back towards the leader. By the time I shot him, the other one was already on me. I felt the weight of his forepaws hit my knees. It was holding me down with one paw while taking swipes at me. It shredded my clothes and scratched my body. The pawing of my belt whisked away my scanner. I positioned the t-ray barrel against its head and squeezed the trigger. It was gone. The claws withdrew from my knee. I picked up the scanner. It wasn't working after the toss to the floor. I looked around for more beasts. None were in sight.

I went to Soya and pulled her closer to the wall for protection. I was exhausted. Our kits had medicine that could stop my knees from bleeding so I poured it on with disinfectant. I didn't know if the creatures had germs or disease fatal to us. I replayed the unbelievable struggle in my mind and realized I was lucky to have beaten them this time. Still, if this was the worst they had, we could still get our job done.

Soya regained consciousness.

She asked, "Wollen, are you all right?"

"My knees are cut." I explained to her what had happened. Afterwards, she bandaged my knees. The distractions had delayed our mission. Soya attempted to put her glasses back together. She couldn't. The communication devices were still operational from her to the ship and back. After a short rest, we returned outside. We needed to follow the mud flow outside rim to avoid structures. We downloaded directions to the shuttle.

After we found the rim, we walked along it as far as we could. We saw more structures, but we didn't bother to explore. We came upon bloated wiggling four-legged creatures. Soya sprayed them. She wasn't taking any chances. In one area, we saw dead creatures wearing clothes. We supposed these were the intelligent creatures responsible for the structures. As we neared a group of structures, we saw more creatures skulking in the shadows. It was dark by then. Soya and I tried to spray them but they were too far away.

Soya said, "Let's call these two-legged creatures, grubs."

I asked, "Why grubs?"

She said, "They remind me of hard to find grubs in my mother's garden."

I said, "Fine."

Our t-rays provided the utility of a light source. If we pushed another button, a weaker, but luminous ray appeared that did not destroy things. We set them on spray to see the holes and turns along the ridge. We ran into more remnants of structures. The cultivation process had pushed many structures against the rim.

Soya suggested, "We should keep moving as fast as possible, and stop now and then to take samples." We only needed small clods to take back for analysis. We were making good time. She and I speculated on why the mud hadn't covered everything. I blamed the structures or something else put in place by the inhabitants for causing the open spots. Soya believed it had to do with the mix we used to gather the liquid up to the sky. Our thoughts were fully on the discussion. We were eager to get back to the lab with our data so we could pass it on and decipher the problem more thoroughly. Our preoccupation is what allowed the next event.

Soya had climbed down the rim, trying to avoid a precarious looking structure. I was right behind her. As she reached the bottom, a grub came out. It was dirty looking, smelled horribly, and was making a low humming sound. She saw it at the last moment and dove away towards the ground. I saw it all as I was coming down. I yelled down to her to find out if she was okay. She hadn't the time to answer. Slipping down to the ground, I saw the slow moving grub jump on her.

I moved towards them. I kicked at the creature on top of Soya. It was trying to bite her. She was screaming and slapping at it. My kicks enabled her to escape from under it. Two creatures came up behind me. One grabbed my jacket collar, pulled me down, and dragged me on my back towards the structure. I called out to Soya, "Run back to the shuttle!" She didn't turn and run. Soya reset the t-ray to the most powerful level. She hurriedly sprayed the first attacker as they dragged me into the structure. I watched as she turned around towards me and sprinted towards my captors.

I twisted around to break their grip. It didn't matter how much I struggled. They held on tight and pulled me into the structure. In the first room, I saw many grubs. The smell was much more fetid.

They threw me on a pile of bones in the corner and promptly surrounded me. Soya entered the room with her t-ray prepped to blast. I heard her calling out, "Wollen, Wollen." She had to locate me before she could blast away. I raised my feet high in the air to kick at my captors. Slowly they moved in closer. Two of them had knives. My already cut knees were no match for their swinging knives. I felt the first cut and then the second.

Soya saw the grubs huddling around me. She sprayed around to the left and to the right. The t-ray hit the grubs, and they misted away from the direct hits. Pushing her way through, she jumped in the air, twisting her body so she landed over me, facing the hungry grubs. Her crash made the pile of bones give way. They popped and cracked as some broke or knocked against other ones. This surprised the knife-wielding pair. They stepped back and paused. That was the split second Soya needed. She had positioned herself so the enemy was in front of us. She set the t-ray on spray and fired forward. It was over in a blink. We were the only living beings left. The grubs injured me so badly that I couldn't use one leg. Her heroic acrobats and the beating had left Soya bruised. The stench of rotting meat covered us after rolling around in the bones. The loss of blood made me pale and weak.

Soya grabbed my arm and pulled me upright. She put her arm around me so I could at least hop on the other leg. We made it outside the structure and back to the rim. I crawled gingerly to the top. We needed to find shelter for safety, and rest for recuperation. We were both worried that we might never make it back to our craft. With superior weapons and detectors not being enough, we had become panicked fugitives.

There I was, Wollen, the lead scientist, faced with indescribable hostility. Nothing had prepared me for it, no matter how much disdain I had for this primitive world. This place pulled us down to its level, the level of kill or be killed. We had succumbed to an uncivilized world we had most likely created.

The wind was blowing. We had no bandages left in our kits. Soya squeezed a small amount of disinfectant on my wounds. She tore off a piece of her shirt to wrap my legs.

Soya filed a report with our orbiting ship. She described the two-legged grubs. She let them know how dangerous and aggressive they had been. They advised us to go back to our shuttle so we could medicate and bandage my cuts. They suggested any other approach would most likely lead to death and failure of our mission and surmised we had enough samples from this area to get results.

We heard a low buzz. It sounded familiar. It was the flying creatures or something like them from before. I was sitting with an open wound partially wrapped with Soya's shirt. I recalled the earlier attack when we first left the shuttle.

Soya said, "It will not be so easy this time with the lack of wind at the top to save us."

She tugged at my sleeve and commanded, "Move it!" I had to use the other leg to get away or we couldn't make it. The pain was unbearable for the first few steps and the wounds bled. After a while, I blocked out the pain. The sky was getting brighter. It would make our escape easier. We would make it. We had to.

A loud buzzing sound from the swarm traveled with a strong wind through the trees. It was seeking us out. My arm was completely black. I tasted and felt small things in my mouth. I reached up to protect my eyes. My nostrils filled with crawling legs. I gagged from the rush into my throat. They were ferocious, fearless, and mindless. The feeding frenzy had begun. Small sucking, stinging bites penetrated our clothes. During the first attack, Soya became a hazy figure in front of me leading the way. Then I couldn't see her at all. They turned into a black cloud swarming around us. It would have been too dangerous to spray them. Besides, the t-ray design did not include spraying air that contained thousands of tiny devils. I felt the fuzziness in my head as a tingling feeling spread down to my knees turning them numb. My body was in shock, and my brain shut off. They sucked my blood out of almost every pore. On my way down, I muttered "Soya, Soya." She couldn't hear me. The bloodsuckers had taken her out first. We were finished!

CHAPTER TWENTY

Shocked, I couldn't believe the screen. It felt like hours had passed after the others had gone to bed. I searched for the locations of other forts while dozing off and on. I mapped out in my mind how to get to the closest fort after taking a closer view via satellite. The zoom view showed signs of towns and buildings. Everything else had become giant plowed up fields. I looked for a big rock or hill that could be an identifying landmark. That is when I noticed a flicker on the motion detector. Maybe someone had a plane and was flying in the air to rescue us. I hadn't completely given up being with or finding others. Especially since other forts were inhabited. Underlying those thoughts of hope was the worry that maybe none of them could be trusted. Maybe no contact was the answer. My youth and naiveté wouldn't let me believe the worst.

A blip was moving across one sector close to our location. A digital read out on the screen bottom warned, "Unknown craft registration, system cannot identify." The letters were red and blinking. Feeling the strangeness, short hairs stood up on my body.

KK was better at operating the system. I needed her help. I switched on the intercom and yelled. "KK, come to the watch room now!" She jumped up and looked at the camera, waved and yelled, "Okay, Brock." Without question, she came running. Tim and Maria also woke up. Tim didn't want to hurry anywhere so he and Maria took off towards the kitchen and game room.

When KK arrived, I pointed at the screen. She immediately took the command console and zoomed in on the craft. She was a natural at this stuff. It was that or our new powers included skills or the brainpower to master technology. After a few seconds, I heard my first cuss words from the army brat. She suggested it was the alien craft mentioned in the blog from the mountains. It was so small we couldn't determine the shape, but we could see it didn't have wings. It showed that its flight began at the Chicago zoo. It was moving straight towards our location.

I wondered if this was the invasion force sent to wipe the rest of us out or take us away for slavery and medical experiments. It was one thing to read about an invasion by aliens but something else to see their craft heading towards our sanctuary.

For once, I had no answers. This was above me now. KK would have to be the one to initiate action. I had reached my limits. She wanted me to set all detectors on motion detection. I had done that. She said, "We should get Tim and Maria and find the cache of weapons as soon as possible." I called out to Tim to come to the watch room. He was in the dining room eating cereal again. When he and Maria arrived, I told them we needed to find the weapons cache. KK stayed at the console watching with relentless intensity. She dug into the online help files on the system looking for more information on how to defend the fort. She soon found the information about hidden escape hatches, weapons, locks, poison gases, and lastly the fort destructor bomb or FDB as abbreviated in the help text.

The FDB, once set, would blow up the entire complex. The FDB system had its own power supply. Maybe,

Home Fort Ten had used the FDB rather than surrendering to potential cannibals.

Triggering small explosions outside the hatches would allow the use of a hidden escape tunnel. It would clear away the dirt or the rock cover concealing the hatch. No one had counted on another layer of mud. The explosives might not clear the way. That would be okay for KK and me since we'd be able to slip right through the walls. Maria and Tim couldn't follow. A remote box resembling a television remote control could turn on the FDB and the escape hatch explosions. It had a number for each hatch and a big button for the FDB. A safety pin on each button prevented accidental firing. We had to find the remote box.

KK learned the alarm system could be set to monitor all portals into the complex, including those hard to find. Working with the online help system, she discovered where the remote box was stored. Having aliens at our front door, made her more willing to dig in.

Tim didn't take long to find the weapons. They were near the front entrance. He hurriedly unwrapped his arm and stretched it out. He grabbed two small pistols. Maria remained unarmed. I grabbed two rifles, grenades, and one pistol. I checked for bullets in the pistols. We took them back to KK. She said, "Get more grenades and haul the other weapons to the kitchen freezer. Bust up the others so they wouldn't work." Tim loved destroying the barrels and triggers. That is until a gun accidentally fired. The shot sent echoes through the hallway. Maria burst out crying. Tim took off and hid behind the reception desk. He wasn't so smart, but he had a streak of cuteness in him.

After finishing our weapon chores assigned to us by KK, I went to the commander's quarters. There in the wall, behind a special sliding panel, I found a fire extinguisher. Behind the extinguisher, I found the remote box held in place with spring-loaded clamps. On the side was a sign in large yellow letters, "Handle with Care." It was a heavy gray metal box as big as a toaster. The buttons were marked and covered with a clear plastic cover. The lock-down pins were very visible. I returned to the watch room and showed the box to KK. She said, "Look for the battery compartment and fresh batteries." After finding the panel for the batteries, I took them out. I dug around in the drawers and cabinets until I found a cabinet labeled "Supplies." There were batteries sitting in a recharge cradle with a small green light. I loaded the charged ones in the remote box.

KK let Maria and Tim return to playing. KK's eyes were showing their whites more than usual. She showed me how much nearer the craft had come. We both knew this would not be a friendly visit and it would be our biggest challenge. We'd have to take full advantage of our new powers. We both felt the nearness of non-humans as the ship came closer, then hovered. Every breath we took had a foreign taste making us more panicky. It was as if we were detecting poison.

Out of nervousness, fright, and the need to touch someone else, I went to KK grabbed her hand. She moved closer. Our breathing was in cadence. We hugged. It was the first time we had come together while awake. My mind wrapped with hers. We had joined into something neither of us had experienced before where our combined energies welded together for a moment. We were sharing thoughts, but more than that, we had only one thought between us. Our individuality was in question. We could see things, feel things, and smell things far away. It felt as if we had been together forever. Our mind's eye knew to search in the sky for the alien ship. We found a ship. It wasn't in space. We had seen it in the watch room. We knew two aliens were coming for us.

They did not have our human shape. Their eyes were larger then human eyes. I detected two small limbs that could have been arms but they hung limp as if not used.

They were tall and broad. It was in a way comforting to know there were only two. Their numbers could have been in the hundreds or thousands. It was as if we had a telescope with pictures and our minds had become a phenomenal reservoir of information. We had to trust our senses, because without speaking, we had the same knowledge. We broke apart.

KK stared into my eyes. She had the nicest smile. I smiled back with the same knowing expression. We had discovered another power. It was a valuable tool for survival. We had shared minds long enough to understand each other fully. Our care for one another had changed into oneness that left no doubt, distrust, or miscommunication possible. We realized this new power truly extended our look-feel. Our coming together enabled it to grow stronger.

CHAPTER TWENTY-ONE

I woke up when I felt something gnawing into my cut. It was a small brown creature. I gathered enough strength to push it away and spray it. The small flying creatures blanketed my body. I rolled on the ground to smash as many as I could. The cloud of creatures flew off me and then quickly returned. Drops of blood from the bites covered me. I felt helpless. Wind driven rain started to fall with hard stinging drops. It was enough to drive the creatures away from Soya and me.

My cuts were throbbing. My knees were still in pain from the skirmish with the grubs. The big claw that had knocked me down earlier scratched my face horribly. I still had the will to live.

Soya had the same amount of fighting power. We were saving millions of lives on Hight. Reaching out for her hand, I pulled myself up. We knew what to do. I, with all my injuries, would have to keep up with her. She forged ahead faster than before. She carried the samples in case I didn't make it. The closer we were to our shuttle, the faster her pace. I was falling farther and farther behind. She had the right priorities. We might not win in another battle with the smallest or largest of threats. One of us had to get back to the shuttle. She was the strongest and the least injured. Rain soaked the dried mud, making it difficult to walk. I might have only been ten minutes away from the shuttle when I fell, so I crawled for a short time then laid down. I rolled onto my back where the rain splattered on my face. It created big spats of mud that splashed into the air then covered my body. It was as if the mud was claiming me. My spirit was dying as I lay there wondering what else would come along to take a piece of me. The loss of blood, coldness, and fatigue was catching up with me. I passed out.

When I woke up, I couldn't believe it. I was in my bunk on our small shuttle. Soya was standing over me. She had gotten to the shuttle and dug out our tools for expeditions including a power sled used to collect large samples. She was dedicated and couldn't leave me behind. On her own, she had taken the sled from the shuttle, and used it to carry me back. It was unbelievable to be back under light in the safety of our shuttle. After she washed me, she medicated my wounds, which included special radiation treatment that sped up the healing of tissue.

Soya sent data from our samples to our orbiting ship. She received orders to go to the next site on the planet. We planned to be more careful where we landed this time. To be less vulnerable we knew we needed to scan the area thoroughly while hovering and searching for the high ground. I got up after a few hours. After eating and drinking, I let her know I was ready to go. She acted surprised. I saw the worried look on her face so I comforted her by saying, "I will be okay." Needlessly, I reminded her how important each day meant to the project. She went to the control room and input the startup commands to take us to the area designated by the Hightians above. Before we took off, we looked outside to where our guards had met their end. Standing in the clearing were the huge gray beasts with a curling appendage coming from their heads. We knew they were something tougher than we would have expected. I was tempted to spray them. Regretfully, we couldn't go into battle with our landing craft. When we finally finish clearing this planet of these local pests, the universe will be a safer place.

CHAPTER TWENTY-TWO

We watched the zoomed screen showing our area as it flashed a warning showing the unknown craft. KK let out a small yelp that got my attention. The craft was still heading towards us. KK opened her email to let the other forts know we had detected movement. She also mentioned the vision of two aliens on the ship. That was the first time we let anyone have a hint on how we had changed. Home Fort Three answered back. They could see the object, too. Home Fort Nineteen didn't reply this time. Home Fort Three never asked how we knew there were only two aliens so we assumed they knew about our powers because they had found theirs. Home Fort Nineteen may have become suspicious because we were sure about the number of aliens. It may have been a danger sign. They had gone silent.

I reminded KK of our old motto, take it slow, and be careful. I called Tim and Maria to the watch room. They could tell from my voice that it wasn't the time to rebel. Tim was playing pinball and Maria was periodically hitting the side causing it to tilt. When they arrived, we sat on the floor.

KK kept glancing at the moving ship on the screen. I

suggested, "If the aliens or the cannibals outside discover us, we might have to travel to Home Fort Fourteen." I assigned Tim to stay with Maria, protect her, and help her escape if we had to change our plans. Tim took the assignment with unaccustomed resignation.

KK said, "We'll have to put together the food, water, clothes, and weapons necessary to make a 200-mile journey. There will be no provisions on the outside." After volunteering to pull together what we would need next, I got out the map before the alien attack. Then showed them which way we'd have to travel when we left. I warned, "It wouldn't be easy."

KK laid out a floor plan of our fort. It was a big plan with colored letters and symbols. The emergency escape hatches were marked with big red Es. The other hatches and main entrance had big green Es. Each room had letters identifying what it was. D was for the dining room. K stood for the kitchen. It was easy to understand because non-government experts created it. Tim pointed at the one marked with a G and stated that must be the garden. I told him, "You are right." That seemed to get him more interested. KK and I planned to get Tim and Maria out through the center hatch. It was the only safe one for them. Then again, we thought the aliens might not find us. I had a feeling that was unlikely. My intuition was telling me that fate was calling us to a rendezvous with two devils from another world.

I rushed to the kitchen with Tim and Maria and loaded up small packets of food. We needed light things that were less prone to spoiling. I purposely looked for dried food in boxes and bags. We put them out in sets of four so everyone would have the same amount to eat and carry. It was impossible to carry enough water for the long trip. The chosen food was lighter so we could cover more days with it. We accepted that fasting would be necessary. We had to make the journey searching for water along the way. I took Maria's portion of food and split it up between us.

She couldn't carry as much. I found bags in the laundry to hold the food. Tim carted the food to the watch room. That took care of the food. Maria followed along. I gathered up clothes, including raincoats, and blankets. These I put in heavy plastic bags I found in the kitchen. We could keep them dry while dragging them on the ground with small cords tied to our hands or waist. If we had to, we could let them go.

I returned to the watch room several times to deliver the clothes and then I went back and got the last two bags of food and water with Tim. KK had become the queen bee. She was the brains of our troop for this operation. I'd given up the role of leader. I didn't enjoy relinquishing control, but I recognized I had to wait for a better time to reestablish my position.

KK looked over the weapons. She decided Tim would get a small handgun. I was to pick up grenades, a rifle, and gas pellets. She planned to take the same. I looked at everything we planned on taking and knew it was too much. KK agreed. She said, "Forget gas pellets, especially since they could cause us problems." Next, we cut the food supply in half. KK had me get the map of all the different fort locations.

KK found a way for Maria and Tim to stay close to the center hatch. They were to make themselves comfortable in a small closet with the supplies and weapons. KK and I would bait the invaders into the garden where an escape tunnel existed. We would blow the hatch although we didn't need to. KK suggested it would be a way to ensure the invaders couldn't follow us. She was showing off her intelligence. At the time of blowing the hatch, Tim and Maria could escape through the center hatch. We would take our supplies and weapons to the escape hatch. If the hatch didn't clear from the charge, our powers would allow us to get out. This plan counted on us keeping the remote box. KK would arm the fort destructor bomb after escaping. We would have to be far away from the fort. I pictured the entire scenario in my head and the pieces fell together.

KK interrupted our activities. In a wild scream, she yelled, "Brock, Brock!" Then she screamed, "Tim and Maria run to your closet!" I looked at the screen and saw why she had panicked. The alien ship flew straight to our site. It was landing on top of us. A big cloud of dust blurred the picture as a blast from the ship dried the mud. Our entire complex vibrated. We heard things fall in different areas. The motion cameras in the different rooms were crazily tracking the items that were falling and rolling. We watched as each room screen displayed snapshot views of activity. In one room, a large mirror fell. In the kitchen, a broken water pipe was spraying water all over. The garden room turned into a blur of dust as air from the ship above blew down into it. In a matter of minutes, our fort fell apart. The engineers of this structure hadn't expected it to be a landing site for a large and heavy spaceship. If the entire place was not noisily vibrating, I would've believed we were watching a sci-fi movie.

We hugged and felt the heat from aliens above us. We also detected more trouble heading our way, a large group of humans. There were too many of them to be from our small town. KK guessed they were from a nearby government base ten to twenty miles away. They must have spotted the aliens' ship as it cruised towards us.

CHAPTER TWENTY-THREE

Soya found the high ground for our next research area. She called out, "Wollen, check the monitors for creatures." I looked into the viewing screen. There were life forms on the landing zone and others in the distance. I expected the landing would kill those few blimps on my screen. We hovered for quite a while. The distant life forms started moving towards our shuttle. I couldn't tell what type of creatures they were. I warned her that there were others coming our way.

Soya immediately landed on the mound. I tried to get up, but I could hardly move. The wounds had made me stiff and clumsy. My reflexes were slow. I scanned the landing zone and to my surprise, the life forms remained below us. I wondered how they had survived the heat and pressure from our craft. Soya dressed in her gear and was ready for the outside trek. She had my outfit in her hands and helped me put it on. I hobbled over to the door leading to the outside. She grabbed the sled she used before and said I could ride it until it ran out of power. We had settled on a more conservative survey that wouldn't take us so far away from our craft. We moved down the ramp to the ground.

She loaded supplies and our t-rays. We thought nothing on this planet of hostiles including the strange biting flying creatures, predators, and large gray creatures could defeat us. Regardless, we were ready to strike first at the slightest movement. My injuries would hinder us, but it wouldn't stop us from accomplishing our mission. If we didn't get this planet inline for the zirns, many Hightians would suffer.

As I hit the surface, Soya was scanning the surroundings. She notified me that the creatures were getting closer. The ones at our landing site still showed, but I couldn't see them outside the shuttle. Soya came down with the sled. I sat on it as Soya pulled and steered as it floated over the ground. Again, I warned, "Soya the creatures are approaching." She pulled me down the hill. We reached the rim of mud and scrambled away as fast as possible. The creatures were close. I said to her, "We'd better stand and fight." We found a crevice to slide into and we put our t-rays on powerful spray. Soya had her eyes focused towards the hill. She gripped the t-ray so tightly that her hand turned a different color. Her preparation for battle was completed. I was lucky to have her by my side. She had a lot of strength and a spunky fighting spirit.

The first few came over the hill. Soya took aim and fired. They were standing upright. They were grubs. Others had climbed on the shuttle trying to open it. We couldn't shoot them because we would've damaged the shuttle. After Soya's shots, the grubs backed out of range. They spread out while encircling us. This was the same tactic used earlier. Based on the scanners, there were hundreds of them. The first few Soya sprayed were dirty looking and partially clothed. The grubs were a primeval hunting pack led by a thinking being. They outnumbered and surrounded us.

Soya reasoned aloud, "We had better get back to the shuttle." I agreed. We left the sled there. We let go of our supplies.

I attacked the ones by our shuttle. Shortly after my first shot, we heard the first loud bang. The grubs had a primitive weapon, shooting projectiles. There were at least two of them. Soya fired back. I stood up above the crevice and drew fire. Lucky for me, they were too far away. Soya spotted both shooters and moved to get out of sight. The shots were sporadic. Soya moved slowly towards the shooter directly in front of me. She had to stand up to get a clear spray. The shooter let another shot go. Soya stood up and fired. The spray did the job. The other shooter spotted Soya. When she stood up, he shot her in the arm. Soya dropped her t-ray and fell to the ground trying to retrieve it. I shot towards the shooter to keep him down while Soya retreated. The wound wasn't serious.

Since we were in no shape to ambush someone, and the circle of grubs surrounding us was getting tighter and denser. We ran for the shuttle. I slid over the crevice. Soya followed. The shooter immediately fired at us. Luckily, he continued to miss. We stood up and took off running. My bleeding knees and legs were hurting. I had to get to the shuttle. Soya was far ahead. She scrambled to the hill top just before the shuttle. A loud roar filled the air. It was the grub's battle cry. There were hundreds coming towards us from every direction. Soya fell to the ground firing her t-ray. She sprayed one wave of grubs, another wave followed right behind. They had gaunt faces with eyes radiating hate and anger. Again, I questioned if they knew we were the ones that did this to them or if this was their natural state. Soya kept in contact with the orbiting command ship. She reported, "We are aborting the scouting trip because of immediate extreme danger."

We had the path to the shuttle cleared except for the ones that had climbed onto the sides. Soya gave the command to the shuttle to lower the ramp. She carefully sprayed a couple grubs close to the shuttle. The others behind and to the side were getting closer and closer. We heard their growls, yells, and thudding footsteps behind us. We smelled their putrid odor.

Soya was on the ramp shooting back and toward the side making sure she didn't hit me. I was limping and still bleeding with every step. After falling down, I crawled to the ramp. Soya grabbed my arm with no regard for her wounded and bleeding arm. She pulled me up. I saw the final door open to the shuttle. We were almost safe.

The whole world shivered and wobbled as the shuttle tilted to one side. I couldn't keep my balance on the ramp. I didn't make it to the last door. Instead, Soya and I rolled down into a crack in the ground, or what we thought was the ground. The pursuers saw what was happening to the shuttle and retreated. It was tipping over. Our landing site had given way. I was confused and dizzy. The crashing sounds drowned out the loud growls from the grubs. Soya and I fell into a chamber. Above us, a large dense cloud of dust was rising to the sky. We heard the swooshing from the air and the noise from the rocking and bouncing movement of our craft. We were stunned, covered with a layer of dust, choking, and frozen with fright. When the ground collapsed, the grubs on shuttle must have met their end. Soya and I were lucky to escape away from the danger. The entire event only lasted minutes but time seemed to slow down. We saw everything in slow motion.

The debris and dirt partially buried me. I sat up. The dust rolled off along with small chunks of dirt and rocks. Soya looked like a mound of dirt. Her left leg was shaking. I yelled out for her. She turned over. Soya asked, "What happened?" We both knew no answer was forthcoming as soon as she asked it. I wondered aloud, "Where are we?"

Meanwhile, above us, the shuttle had broken up and fire was consuming it. We could hear noises from the grubs coming closer as they yelled victory chants in unison. We moved away from the crevice because anything above could see us.

I was aware it would only be a matter of time before the foraging grubs above would find this cave-in. We couldn't go back to the surface. As we moved, Soya was briefing the on-orbit command. When she described the condition of our shuttle, the tone of their response changed. We were to stay put until rescued. That was, assuming our leaders would attempt one. Shortly after that communiqué, they shut off contact. Things were happening so fast we didn't have the time to worry about the Saviors abandoning us.

This planet had been one terror after another. I believed the few samples we collected made our mission a failure because they would be insufficient. Our forays outside the landing craft had turned into nightmares. Our confidence and presumed superiority had turned into injury, pain, fright, and death. We found ourselves in a fissure in the surface that had cracked under the weight of our shuttle. We were running like rodents from exterminators. This planet was a jungle of madness way beyond what anyone had expected. Our world didn't have these constant threats. We had centuries of scientific control that had eliminated perilous dangers. That is why our guards didn't have the edge like the wild beings. They were inexperienced and weak. Soya and I were of the same ilk. We didn't have what it took to be the dominant ones even with our t-rays. The guards and t-rays had been an archaic tradition that was a target of ridicule. Our biggest mistake was under estimating the power of primitive beings. The uncaring, single-minded approach we had taken had caught up with us.

CHAPTER TWENTY-FOUR

Tim and Maria were in the closet. The ship landed and turned its engine off. The motion cameras were still. Some were out of commission due to the amount of activity. We tasted the dust as it seeped its way into every crevice in every room. KK sat staring at the screens. She let the other forts know we were having personal contact with aliens. After sending out the warning to all, she turned and ordered me to grab the weapons and prepare to escape. I lifted our bags onto the table so I could grab them and run if we had to.

We waited to see what else would happen. KK came close. We hugged with our eyes closed. It was strange again. The knowledge we were sharing wasn't a vision; it resembled more of an intuition. We couldn't see what was going on, but we knew it was happening. While we were hugging, the aliens were leaving the ship. We knew that and we knew in the periphery groups of humans were moving towards them and the ship. There were hundreds of them. They seemed to have leaders giving commands. These weren't the small group of cannibals encountered in the town. They were organized militants banded together in gangs for protection and survival. Our fort would be a luxury resort for them with food and weapons. We would have been a few children, to smash and toss, literally, to the side. As we saw the aliens hurrying back to their ship, shaking accompanied by loud creaking and popping noises, interrupted our look-feel. The lights were flickering off and on. KK yelled into the intercom, "Tim, be ready to get out."

The sounds turned into loud crashing. Lights went out. Screens lost all pictures. The computer screen blinked with zigzag lines then gave off a small poof sound and went off. I smelled smoke. We were in the dark. The fort fell silent for one short moment. Then like the noise and shaking from a diesel train engine hitting the side of a building, our world exploded like doom-night. The tremors made my stomach queasy. I had the same feeling when I first detected the aliens. KK and I clung to each other. Our bond had grown stronger in the last few days. We fell to the floor grunting as we hit it. Rolling together and hugging tightly let us know the ship above was in yellow and blue flames, spewing out smoke. It was a peculiar feeling knowing that closing our eyes gave us more vision than when they were open. The chanting militants had surrounded our hill. They were raising and lowering their arms, swinging their weapons in the air.

I reached out for our bags and guns. I already had a belt with grenades and a handgun. KK was doing the same. She held on to the remote box. It was the key to our plan. We knew our fort was penetrated. Our new sense was sharper than ever. We had gotten used to recognizing the nuances and stopped trying to deny it was real. We could smell the fumes from the ship's fire. Closing my eyes, I saw my path in the dark. KK did the same. The aliens had no way of knowing their chemicals from their strange universe had mixed with our laws of physics to change us.

Our tuned senses could tell the aliens were closer to the reception room. We weren't far away. The watch room was so close we could actually hear doors open from one to the other. Although we could see the path to follow, the debris presented another problem. We couldn't always discern when something was in our way. As we opened the door from the command center, we could hear movement in the hallway and reception room. That meant the aliens were coming out, too. We hurried across to the laundry room. As we shut the door, a ray of light flashed behind us. It had to be the aliens. They had a flashlight. After entering, KK tripped on loose blocks lying on the floor. She fell head first, hitting the front of a washing machine. This made a loud booming sound. The aliens had to have heard it. Breaking out in a cold sweat, I expected the aliens would enter.

We had left our tracks in the dust layer in the hallway. Two gruesome aliens were stalking us. They'd know how many were inside but they didn't know if we were armed and dangerous. We saw the light under the door. I whispered to KK, "We'll have to go through the wall to the storage closet on the other side." I grabbed a grenade from my belt, pulled the pin, and placed it carefully on the floor. KK went through first then I followed.

We stood motionless in the closet waiting for the grenade to explode. A loud muffled boom sounded off. We remained quiet while waiting for a sign of life. A light appeared under our closet door. They hadn't fallen for our trap. To our surprise, they didn't enter the closet. They had moved down the hall. KK reached out and hugged me. We knew instantly they were using their light and moving slowly down the hallway past us. They were not moving smoothly. They appeared to be hurt but with the fallen debris in their path, we couldn't tell for sure.

Our plan changed. We couldn't bait them to our escape path towards the garden and away from Tim and Maria. They headed towards the complex center where Tim and Maria were in hiding. I hoped Tim could keep Maria calm. We knew they stopped right at the door where Tim and Marie were hiding. We couldn't stay put any longer. KK went through the wall first and pulled me along. We turned towards the aliens, yelling to distract them. KK kept a hold of me as we passed through the next wall. It was the dining room. We slid through the wall hoping to get ahead of them again. As soon as we passed through, I hugged KK. We perceived the aliens moving back to where we had slipped into the dining room. Our plan was working. Our look-feel showed us much more. There, where the aliens had fallen in, were the militants climbing into the fort. They would soon be in the reception and hallway. The militants' arrival would occupy the aliens' attention.

The aliens made it to where we had gone through the wall. They stood there touching and pushing on it. They couldn't believe we went through the solid surface. From there, they could hear the noises the militants were making. The crazy militants were attacking. Before entering the hall, they fired off an automatic weapon causing bullets to ricochet through the hall. The aliens dropped to the floor to avoid the wild shots. They turned their lights off. We could sense they were alive and close to us. We saw a militant jump down on to the hall floor. A flash came from where the aliens were lying low. The militant exploded into thin air.

We just witnessed the alien capabilities. Their weapons were powerful and fast.

KK suggested, "Let's move to where Tim and Maria are hiding." Her idea was to take them with us through an emergency escape hatch. She knew with both aliens and the militants making their way deeper into our complex, Tim and Maria would have no chance of getting away on their own. With the aliens hiding out waiting to ambush the crazy militants, it was an ideal time to make our move. The trouble was, once we hooked up with them, the jumping through walls would come to an abrupt end.

Slowly, we moved into the commander's quarters. This

put us close to Tim and Maria. KK said, "Let's go for them." We slipped out, moved to the kitchen, out the other wall and into the closet where Tim and Maria were waiting. Tim almost shot us when we came through the wall. KK heard the pistol hammer click and yelled, "It's us." He was dumbfounded with what we had done. He instinctively reached up and touched KK's hand to believe it. Maria was frightened. KK took Maria's hand and pulled her closer to the door. Tim followed behind. She opened the door and looked around the corner. She didn't see a thing. After hearing automatic guns firing, we sat, listened, and waited.

Everything quieted down for a few moments. KK said, "Maria be ready to run." Tim seemed anxious and ready to fight a battle. Her plan would expose them as little as possible while moving from one room to the next, making their way to an escape hatch in the garden.

The next room was the kitchen. KK opened the closet door with Maria standing in front of her legs so KK could hustle her out in front, as they escaped. KK nudged Maria to move farther ahead. That's when things went wrong. Maria took off. She jumped into the hallway and ran towards the kitchen. KK stood stunned for too long of a moment because she heard Maria hit something that responded with movement. A flashing ray of light appeared. Pushing Tim back into the closet, we huddled together.

CHAPTER TWENTY-FIVE

We had no way to go but back into the dark hall. Soya's bleeding was getting worse. I was hurting everywhere on my body from the fall. We needed clean air and most of all rest. We set our t-rays to give us light. The dust, smoke, and fumes from the shuttle's crashing were blinding us and making breathing difficult. The ranting devils above were chasing us. Our chance of escape was limited. We had to move fast to stay out of sight. Our first impression was that the place was nothing more than a harmless cavern. We hoped to find another way out or at least a hiding place. We were unaware the place had inhabitants. First impressions aside, we were still being cautious.

We found a door. Opening it slowly, I noticed movement just ahead of us. With the swirling dust and smoke, I couldn't be sure. Soya shined her t-ray down at the floor as I shined mine ahead into the darkness. There were fresh tracks in the dust. We could tell there were only a few grubs making the tracks. We stood there for a moment trying to decide what to do next. I didn't want to enter a room where I was sure the grubs were waiting. We weren't in battle condition. A loud sound came from the room after we moved away from the door. The enemy had set a trap. This worried me. It meant they knew we were there. They were stalking us.

We heard the grubs from above falling to the floor through the cave-in. They were yelling loudly as they were coming for us. The underground inhabitants were setting traps for us. Behind us, we knew the odds were against us. Ahead, farther on maybe, we would find the place to hide or an escape route. That was the idea until the projectile weapons spewed into the hallway. Soya and I both dropped to the floor. Turning our lights out, we stared towards the entrance where there were flickering. We stayed patient. A grub jumped into view. Soya fired first with my shot a split second afterwards. The grub was gone.

Upright or just lying in the hall waiting wasn't a choice with the wild shooting taking place. I nudged Soya and told her, "We have to make our move now." Standing upright, we followed the wall. We found a door. I entered. I expected they'd come in full force shooting continuously. It had to be the only move left for them. Surely, the fear of dying was not something influencing their behavior. They were typical of all warriors who stood in the face of death where many died and the few remaining conquered.

We were facing personal defeat. Our life's goal was in play on the other three planets. Our brain work had already changed destiny for billions. Hightians would make it through centuries because they had supported our dreams. The Saviors took care of our families really well and our world honored them because they produced us. Yet, we were in a position so far from the security, respect, celebrations, and civility back on Hight that no one there could imagine this in their wildest dreams. We were following through with our dedication. The ignorance that drove us into this predicament was extracting a heavy toll.

Soya left the room. She peeked out the door holding

her t-ray in front. She stepped out all the way, so I followed. We knew where we were going. In our condition, moving quickly wasn't an option. We passed another door. After passing it, I heard it open. Startled, we both turned around to defend ourselves. It was still dark. I didn't see the small grub that had run into my legs. Soya switched her ray to light only. We both watched as the small blond-haired grub ducked into the next door. By this time, the tension had overcome my patience and good reasoning. Soya went in first. She swept the room with her light. I stayed by her with my t-ray poised to fire.

CHAPTER TWENTY-SIX

I waited long enough. KK hadn't moved. The frantic firing was off and on in the hall. I laid on the floor and moved close to the wall on the kitchen side. I slipped through the wall. I saw the aliens searching the kitchen. Maria was most likely hiding where we first found her. I pulled back into the closet to tell KK and Tim.

Tim suggested, "Let's run into the room, guns blazing."

KK said, "We should distract the aliens from the hallway."

I said, "We need to surround them."

KK stayed with Tim. I opened the closet door, ran past the kitchen door into the kitchen pantry. KK was on one side and me the other side. After he heard our shots, Tim was to crawl out the closet door and enter. I cautioned them to make sure they shot the aliens and not me. KK chuckled at that. We were to count to 50 and then attack. I expected a count to 50 was more than enough time for me to get into position. The risk was that the aliens might have enough time to find Maria. We had no choice. At 50, KK slipped through the kitchen wall. We were only seconds apart. She fired towards the aliens. They ducked down behind the large raised center island. I entered from the pantry. They were in between us. My shots followed KK's but I did not have a clear angle. The aliens had no time to respond. Tim entered crawling on the floor then shooting below the center island. His aim was towards their feet. Painful groans followed his firing. I interpreted them to mean Tim had wounded them. KK and I both sank to the floor, next to a wall. Our shots missed them. As planned, Tim retreated through the door and headed towards the garden.

As Tim left, Maria swung open the cupboard door, stepped out, and without pause ran after Tim.

She called out, "Tim." That was more than enough to be noticed. KK and I watched it unfold. Our little Maria took a few steps, the alien jumped up in the air to fire, and in a flash, she was gone. KK shot first. Our shots came too late.

KK returned to the closet. I joined her. We needed to catchup to Tim. Reaching the garden was easy. Tim was there and to our surprise, he had the bag we had given him. He looked at us with puzzlement.

Tim asked, "Where's Maria?"

"The aliens killed her," KK answered.

Tim looked sad for a moment and then his face twisted in anguish.

Emotionally, Tim was the closest to Maria.

He asked, "What are we going to do?"

KK explained, "It is better to escape than to have another confrontation with the aliens." I agreed.

Tim didn't agree and declared, "I'll get them myself."

I reminded him, "You already wounded an alien, and now they are more dangerous than ever. Besides, they are too much for you." His mindset didn't change.

KK jumped in, "You are too important to us for our survival. If we lose you, the two of us couldn't survive."

It took a while, but finally he said, "Okay"

Our look-feel let us know the aliens were on the move and behind them were the regrouped militants. They crowded together with incoherent chanting, using their courage and excitement to regroup for another mass attack. The aliens could kill one after another, but it wouldn't matter. They would continue the wave of bodies until no more existed. Tim's bullets and roaring militants must have prompted the aliens to leave the kitchen no matter how much damage they had suffered.

They were very large panicked creatures moving like wounded animals. They turned and sprayed one set of attackers and then another. The third set of chasers stalled, and then dropped to the floor. This gave the aliens the opportunity to make it to the garden.

KK was digging out the remote box. She pulled out the safety pin and hit the button to explode the escape hatch. A huge muffled explosion jiggled the entire garden. Dust from the beams and ceiling rained down. An alien entered the room. It did not shoot at us. I believe it somehow sensed we were the key to escaping, or they didn't see us in the dust.

After the explosion, I noticed another alien in the room. KK and I moved away from the escape hatch to distract them. The militants rushed into the garden. The militants distracted the aliens. The aliens killed them as they entered. On the fourth wave, the militants wounded an alien. Tim was already at the hatch trying to pull it open.

This was the closest we had been to the aliens. This time they weren't far away, hiding, or envisioned by our look-feel powers. We saw them fully for the first time in person. They wore like uniforms with long hair or fur sticking out all over. At this first sighting, we realized together they were scarier, bigger, and had a detectable air of determination. It only took a short time to avoid the repulsiveness they presented because they planned to kill us.

Tim was still by the hatch, struggling with the handle to get it open. KK and I had to get out but only after Tim began his ascent. Everything was timing at that point. Doing anything early could get us all killed. As Tim finally opened the hatch, a river of dust flowed into the garden. The plume was so large it hid Tim. An alien stopped firing and took notice. The other one fired at the militants as they entered. Tim crawled up the tunnel towards the top hatch. The ablest alien got up and hustled towards the escape tunnel. KK took shots at it, but missed.

We hugged to summon our look-feel. We saw Tim moving up the loose dirt. Then he turned around and noticed the alien chasing him. He fired. At first, the bullets didn't matter. Then, Tim hit his mark.

The alien collapsed back to the ground, sliding down into the garden. As it rolled down, a dust cloud rose. It was dead or near death. The other alien crawled over to it, hid behind it, and continued to fire at the militants. If the alien could hold off long enough, the escape tunnel wasn't far off. The militants stopped attacking in close order. This was a moment of opportunity. Turning around, the alien crawled up the escape tunnel. Daylight shined through the tunnel into the garden. The militants reentered the garden but couldn't see the alien. They moved cautiously towards the tunnel.

KK and I moved up through the wall with our eyes closed. We could tell how far we had to go. Tim was on top waiting for us. We joined him and ran as quickly as we could away from the fort. The aliens had put up a horrific struggle, but the militants were not stopping with an alien still alive. After a few minutes of rest to catch our breath, KK and I hugged tightly. We saw the militants in the tunnel shooting up at the alien.

KK grabbed the remote box with the plastic cover and opened it. She pulled the safety pin out and toggled the FDB switch. As soon as she pulled the switch, the ground trembled. The sound almost equaled the boom of doom-night. The entire hill supported by the complex heaved up into a cloud of dust and debris. It knocked us off our feet.

We lay there frozen, watching the plume of smoke and dust in the sky. The explosion engulfed the fallen inflamed alien ship. It added to the explosion. Tim stood up with a smile on his face because he knew we had killed Maria's murderers. KK was pulling herself up looking for the box.

I asked, "Why do you need it?"

"Being a standard configuration, it could be used at any fort." I wasn't sure what she had in mind.

There were only three Twelves left. Our time in the fort had allowed us to become stronger physically and mentally while our powers had grown. We were definitely a family. We had to keep moving. There could be more militants. Our sanctuary was gone. We had repelled the aliens not knowing what price we'd pay.

A journey lay ahead with 250 miles of savage wilderness. We were the victors. KK and I had tremendous powers. We stopped one more time before leaving the site to remember Maria our little sister again. To make her departure complete Tim yelled back, "Bye Maria." As we walked away, we felt things falling from the sky and believed it to be from the explosion. The Twelves had won again, a joyless victory with the loss of Maria. Doom-night carried on, as it began, with Earth-shaking explosions. We took it slow and were careful.

Part III Aftermath

CHAPTER TWENTY-SEVEN

Many days had gone by since my shuttle had toppled over and threw us into a hole in the ground. Then an explosion spit me out of the escape tunnel. I was still grieving over Soya's death in the subterranean garden. The wounds from the explosion and battles that led up to it were not healing. I was desolate without medicine, food, water, or shelter. I hoped the orbiting ship had a plan to save us. They had powerful scanners and my genetic imprint. Given they valued me; it would be only a matter of time before they came to my rescue. The only counter argument to the entire idea was the surrounding landscape. Zirns covered it. The ship had released the entire crop per plan without regard for the massive uncultivated areas and troublesome natives. The ship's crew did not know how much a difference the zirns would make in this virtual wasteland. They didn't realize the zirn seedlings were more than enough to sustain the planet survivors. The inadequate cultivating had allowed many forms of life to survive and they would consume many immature zirn seedlings. I found it was the only nourishment available.

At first, I, Wollen, didn't want to be a destroyer of my own project. Hunger won out. I was sure the planet inhabitants had discovered the bountiful gifts from space. Gathering the zirn at this stage was exceptionally easy. I ate them as I found them. It was beyond my imagination that the years of work in the lab would end with me surviving from the results of our genius, not like this anyway.

I was still somewhat in shock from the terrible defeat I had experienced in the last few days. The terrain and creatures were all foreign and life threatening. The shuttle's collapse and explosion stretched my composure to its limits. I think I would've gone crazy if it hadn't been for the slight hope of a rescue.

I needed shelter, yet I had no energy nor physical ability to seek it out. When I napped, I worried about the marauding horde finding my weaponless body and ripping it apart. My dreams were nightmares, no longer filled with fantastic delusions on how good things would be.

I wanted to scavenge around the annihilated shuttle to pick up weapons or a communication device. My mind was willing but my body was in no shape to be the supreme invader from outer space. I kept busy by planning to get revenge for the death of my partner and the destruction of our wonderful zirns. With our seedling crop ripped up and wasted on the grubs, we would lose hundreds of thousands of Hightians. My Saviors wouldn't let me down and they would have to help me with my new cause.

I heard faint cries from the grubs, probably searching for me. I found a crevice close to where the blast threw me. It wasn't a perfect fit for me but it had a small overhang for protection from the occasional storms and it was enough to keep me out of sight. I was out of harm's way. I kept things in perspective by shutting out the wants in my life and by concentrating on the simple needs that were being satisfied. However, I never once considered myself lucky for being there.

As I prepared to follow my daily zirn-gathering routine

outside the crevice, a grub struck me with a rock. Unknown to me, the horde was waiting for me to come out of my hiding place. I heard them yelling angrily at me. The first rock hit my leg. The subsequent rocks knocked me out.

I realized how foolish I'd been for believing that hideout would be safe. The grubs had captured me and I was at their mercy. I was sure my life would soon end through a form of merciless torture.

The rock throwing grubs were standing in front of a large group. All were making shrill sounds as if to honor the rock throwers and to share in the assumed benefit of capturing an alien. I watched as they rammed their bodies together while slapping hands above their heads. They were cruel and mean like the striped creatures we first encountered. Every living thing we had discovered so far shared the same traits. It was a big celebration. I was the guest of honor and the main attraction.

Smaller younger grubs came my way to see the monster from space and spit on me. I watched as the ones with long hair left the rowdier larger ones. They meandered over, and then kicked me. They used thick sticks to swing down on me. It was terrifying lying there, falling in and out of consciousness. My mind blocked out the beating they were giving me, for no other reason than to survive and return with a vengeance.

The parade of long haired tormentors finished their torture. I saw the larger ones staring at me with hateful expressions. They wouldn't be as harmless as the others. They were much heavier. My imagination, spurred by fear, was racing with scenarios of my demise.

The first one lifted my leg and dragged me towards a pit. It dragged me close to the edge where another large brute ran up and pushed me down into the pit. I heard sounds of wood breaking as I fell. They were roasting their next meal. After a short while, they had me covered with boards. Through small slits, I could see flashes of torches. I plowed into the ground. The smoke was dense. My thin cover of dirt would only let me survive for a short time. Eventually, I would be rosy red and ready for the feast. What better way to eliminate your alien enemy than to eat it?

CHAPTER TWENTY-EIGHT

We had the aliens off our trail. They had killed or frightened away the militants. We had a plan to find Home Fort Fourteen. New trials lay ahead for us but despite our fatigue and injuries, we were stronger than before. Tim was coming of age. He had shown signs of change and might become more like us. KK and I were learning more and more about our new-found powers. Our minds came closer to being one every time we joined. We expected it to grow into one wordless shared stream of thought with all the powers of our look-feel.

Tim took the lead, setting off towards our new home. KK followed far enough behind so the two of them wouldn't fall into a chasm. I brought up the rear. We became accustomed to the cadence. Tim was being extremely cautious. He was taking it slow and being careful.

We had an aggressive schedule that didn't allow for interruptions or defensive maneuvers. Our plan was to go straight ahead, not worrying about what lay in our path. Without landmarks along the way, finding the fort would be a challenge. It was still our best hope. I was scared the new world had more threats and danger than we could imagine. I found courage enough to carry on with the support of KK and Tim.

The raining debris from the sky wasn't from the fort destructor bomb. It was organic and came from space. At first, KK thought they were weapons or poison spread over the Earth to annihilate the remnants of life. We soon discovered the softness and harmlessness of the small creatures being sprinkled into the horizon. Tim was the first to take a bite out of one and he let us know how tasty it was. KK was leery. She was holding off until I tried it. I followed Tim's lead and gobbled up the entire thing. Afterwards, KK followed along with a small taste.

Having such a needed and ample supply of food falling from space surprised us. Our world was ready for the gift with the new fields of dried mud covering most of it. We, the inhabitants, were in pure glee and rejoiced as our stomachs filled. The cycle of life was restarted and hope for Mother Earth was alive and well. Time would bear witness to how successful the new world would be.

At first, we were quickly racing along, partly from having just escaped the battle and explosions and partly wanting to get to our new home. Our pace slowed after five miles of hiking through the rough terrain. KK had taken the lead from Tim. With her injuries, she set a more reasonable pace.

Our plan called for a straight line to the other fort and so we never thought about having to avoid what may lie ahead. We heard loud moaning and cries from a distance. Our look-feel was stronger than ever. Slowing down we cautiously moved ahead. KK and I thought about coming together to envision what was ahead but decided against it because we felt no immediate danger. Besides, it would slow us down more. As we came closer, the moaning and cries became louder. The feeling in my chest burned from the nearness of others. We couldn't see where the sound was coming from until we walked up to an expansive hole in the mud plain.

Inside it was a human mess of injured trying to crawl out while others fought over the gifts from space. Most were stationary, crying, and moaning in misery. There were many dead bodies strewn about. Carried by a soft breeze, the stench of death whisked up from the hole. The dead were hampering the mobility of those who could move around. They must have been part of a large population caught up in the mudflow. Most of them seemed on the verge of dying. Engaged in the melee, none noticed us peering down. A few had made it to the top. They were weak loners who couldn't take us on and win. There seemed to be no organized control only panic, confusion, and desperation. Where did so many people come from?

Trying to make it through the slaughter pit for the damned would have been ridiculous. Going around the chasm was our best choice. I didn't know what direction to take for the shortest route but I took the lead anyway. We had to travel at least twenty miles a day and more if possible. We didn't want to end up like those below. We found another roadblock. It was a smaller pit leading into the larger pit.

As we shuffled up to the rim and looked below, we immediately pulled back. Below us was a group of cannibals who were using the lame in the pit as a food supply. They had large barbecue pits piled with unlit wood and skewered humans. Tim moved forward to get a better look.

I asked Tim, "Do you have any idea how many are there?"

"No idea."

Our world had turned into pockets of lawless desperation where the small but plentiful supplies from space made no impact on greed and power. This time we didn't have three strolling man-eaters to worry about, but a team of organized hunters and killers. Will they harm us given the number of available victims in the larger pit? I didn't believe we would be welcomed with open arms. More than likely, they'd see us as a threat or just another meal.

We were unaware there were patrols to roundup any newcomers while keeping anyone from escaping. As we moved away to plan our next move, six men came up behind us. They trapped us between the smaller and bigger chasms with no walls to slide through for a convenient escape. Our look-feel hadn't differentiated between them and those in the chasms.

Their leader came forward and sort of grunted for us to move into the smaller chasm. I felt KK's mind reaching out to mine. I felt she didn't want to end up down below in line for the next roasting where we would be outnumbered and imprisoned. It would be our end. She still had her pistol, and I had mine. The patrol wasn't expecting armed visitors. Tim, still holding our only bag of supplies including the FDB and map, was nervously glancing back and forth between our captors. He was ready to strike out as he had with the intruder. All of us were ready to pounce on the unsuspecting patrol.

KK was the first to strike. She fell to the ground to cover the drawing of her pistol. As she looked up with her pistol firing, the first one collapsed. I was in step with her. I sensed the exact moment when she fell so I grabbed my pistol and shot another. Tim slipped behind the third fellow, then ran towards him with all of his might and pushed him off the cliff. The first three were out of action. Three others, caught completely off guard, were slow to react. The fellow behind Tim turned and grabbed him with both hands around his throat. Picking Tim up, he squeezed and swung his body. Our bag of goodies flew from Tim's hands. KK moved towards them but the other guard tackled her. KK's pistol flew forward. I fired a shot at him and missed. It was enough to get his attention. He released KK, stood up, and took off running.

159

CHAPTER TWENTY-NINE

I kept digging trying to avoid the heat. The smoke from the fire was seeping into my lungs. I could barely see through the blazing fire on top of me. There was a ring of chanters around the pit. After a while, I would pass out and never wake. The life of Wollen, scientist and hero of my world, would be over. I remembered how my parents depended upon the extra benefits from my participation in the program. I hoped this failure wouldn't take the benefits away. Then I remembered how crucial this planet was to thousands on Hight. My mind filled with thoughts of escape and revenge.

The hot smoke and heat burned my eyes. The grubs were still around the rim waiting for me to be cooked.

Through the fire's crackling noises, I heard crashing sounds as if someone had fallen into the pit. I blinked from the ashes falling into my eyes. I could no longer see through the fire but instead I heard screaming and more crashes. Still fighting to stay conscious, I glimpsed a grub falling towards me. I wondered if they were jumping in or if someone pushed them.

The fire was burning my clothes. The flames were scorching me. It wouldn't be long before any question I had on any subject would be meaningless. Then, I felt the spray of a liquid smothering the fire. The crashing bodies covered the entire pit. I was smashed down from their weight and the chopped up wood. My resignation to die had taken the spirit out of me and I didn't have enough curiosity or imagination left to conjure up what was happening.

The fire was out. My almost roasted body was immobile. I felt an inkling of relief when I realized things were improving. I felt the grubs being lifted out of the pit. Someone was throwing the wood aside. As the pressure diminished, the dust from the ashes increased. I was coughing loudly because every breath caused me to suck in more ash. The light broke through and gave me a chance to see what had saved my life.

I was astounded but too tired, burned, and wounded to show any surprise. Above me was Onard, who had personally led the rescue team to save me. He knew how valuable I was to Hight. He cleared away the dirt and ash covering me. Onard knew I was alive because the ship above scanned the surface to find me and if I had perished, they wouldn't have picked up my location. I wondered how they made it down to the surface since I had the only shuttle but that was a question for later.

"How are you?" Onard asked. I was in no shape to answer back. I could hardly open my eyes as a way of acknowledging the question. He dug me out then slowly lifted me up. I couldn't stand on my own so they put me on one of our power sleds.

I was high enough in the sled to see the carnage caused by Onard's attack. Onard explained, "We didn't use t-rays. We used shock weapons to send out force waves that turned the inside of their body into jelly." This weapon wasn't as clean as the t-ray, but the range and spread of its ray was much greater. I was down in a hole so they didn't have to worry about harming me. Onard had guards posted around the site to pick off survivors and to ward off new arrivals.

The caretakers did a full analysis on me before moving me to the shuttle. I was slipping in and out of consciousness. A caretaker sprayed me with painkiller so my fear, shock, and pain would go away. After the spray, I couldn't feel the power sled at all. In large contrast from a few minutes before, I was in a dream-like state without worries.

Our medical curative abilities had benefited from the research to create food supplies. Yet, that was another reason we were so overpopulated. We'd not die from diseases or poor healthcare. Longevity increased significantly five times in the last 100 years.

Safely aboard the shuttle, I heard the engines blast off, I promised myself this wouldn't be my last visit to this planet.

Once back on the ship, Onard explained that after the big explosion, the others gave up on finding me. The debris from the shuttle and underground structure interfered with the scanner's ability to find me. It kept returning negative results. After a brief time, they delivered the zirns and recorded as many results as possible.

The shuttle was a gift from the ever-watching Saviors. Early on, they'd recognized the danger and sent a smaller ship to help eradicate the vermin. The smaller ship was faster than our big ship and it had a shuttle like ours. Before the ship returned to base, Onard insisted they perform another scan. They discovered my profile, he gathered a crew to take the newly arrived shuttle down to rescue me. No one objected. Given the level of death on Hight and the likelihood thousands or millions more would succumb, risking a few more wasn't a worry. Losing another shuttle may have been a bigger risk.

The rescue was successful and the Saviors on Hight had witnessed it. Being in charge of morale, they promptly posted video news flashes throughout our planet to let everyone share in the small triumph. Stories like these reduced the risks of total chaos. I caught a broadcast and found it to be such good news that my spirit lifted. That was strange because I should have felt happier already since they rescued me. Perhaps knowing the world shared my fortunate event was enough to give me the push I needed to get back to my thoughts of revenge.

Part IV Voyage

CHAPTER THIRTY

KK crawled over on her knees and elbows to the man holding Tim and bit his leg. She bit hard on his calf. He didn't release Tim. Without pause, she snaked around his leg and bit him as close as she could on the inside of his upper thigh. This was enough to make him let go. Tim was unconscious. I fired one shot at him wounding him in the shoulder and knocking him down.

I couldn't ward off the other guard. He hit me in the head with his fist. I fell to my knees semi-conscious. He was winding up with another punch when KK pushed him towards me. Her push was enough to make him stumble forward into me. The collision knocked me all the way to the ground. I was regaining enough awareness to react to our situation. With me on the ground, the guard turned back towards KK. I barely remember firing my pistol. He fell to the ground. The other wounded guard stood up holding his shoulder and ran. We were in no shape to chase him.

Tim, our courageous young fighter, wasn't moving. KK rushed over to him to see if he was alive. He was alive. Through the dirt on his neck, I could see the red bruises. We didn't know how long we'd have before the wounded guard would return or another patrol would find us. I rolled the dead guard bodies into the chasm. KK searched for her pistol. She had me pick up Tim's fallen bag.

The unconscious and limp Tim was too heavy to carry. After finding her pistol and without a word KK grabbed one of Tim's wrists. I did the same. We pulled him far enough away from the rim so the patrols wouldn't find us. We scuffed up Tim's butt, yet it was better than facing another gang of toughs.

We got quite a distance away. Tim's backside was scratched up and bleeding. The big chasm circumvention caused us to be way off our original path, not to mention the time lost. In this case, our poor Tim might never be the same. No telling how much damage the guard had caused to his neck, throat, or brain. We found a low-lying spot where we could peek out by lifting our heads and where others couldn't see us next to Tim.

Tim stayed out for more than an hour. When he first opened his eyes and tried to talk, we couldn't understand anything he said. He was speaking a foreign language. After babbling on for ten minutes, he spoke English. I asked him about the foreign language gibberish. He looked at me with an expression I hadn't seen from him before. His face took on a peaceful look and his demeanor changed to someone with authority, wisdom, and power.

KK and I felt a significant difference in him. We thought he was acting this way due to the beating and choking. After a half hour, we knew Tim had joined with us by acquiring our new powers. The difference was he seemed to be more than us. He had gained an aura so strong that we felt it from twenty feet away. We didn't know what it meant. We understood Tim was no longer the weak and immature whipping boy we had carried all this time.

I asked Tim, "Do you feel different?" He answered,

"Our world is the light, and darkness will never reign." After that answer, I didn't bother to ask him anything else. We thought he had tapped into a stream of intelligence far above the reality we were reaching. KK and I worried he might be too far out of the here and now and would endanger himself and us. If being something wiser and stronger than KK and me was bad, we would have to wait and see.

Tim stood up and walked towards Home Fort Fourteen. He didn't tell us to follow. He expected us to follow. His aura of power didn't enslave us through force, but made us feel assured and safe. My mind was struggling with this change in leadership. During the trip, Tim was the reckless irresponsible child I protected, cared for, and controlled. Now he wasn't Tim the child but Tim the leader. As I was struggling with the change, Tim turned back towards me. I heard a message in my mind. "Worry and pride are brother and sister in need of a father's helpful hand." Somehow, he knew.

KK accepted his influence and mentioned, "Tim is sharing the new wealth of the world with us." By not resisting, she was more in touch with the direction of our powers. I had become the odd man out. She was a follower, with sporadic spans of leadership. I followed behind them, not knowing how I would fit into the future.

Tim held up his hand for us to stop. He sensed something ahead. KK and I had no sensations. This would be our first experience with Tim pulling the strings. We didn't know what to expect. We heard the wind coming from the direction of Home Fort Fourteen. The wind unexpectedly roared very near us. It contained a small twisting funnel with large pieces of debris. If we had kept going forward, the funnel would've trapped us in that fury with no chance of escaping in one piece. Tim had demonstrated one of his new abilities. I was becoming a true believer.

We had left the cannibal camp behind us. It was good

to get away without a scratch. Once again, our small troop had beaten the odds. Every time we battled, our trust and closeness became stronger. KK and I had almost become one sentient being after the challenges. Our hugging allowed our minds to wander the unseen together. Our power to sense others close by and far off grew with each day. We'd been at the point of feeling or knowing what the other person was thinking. This was something not fully developed. Our evolution, spurred on by would-be conquerors, was still in its infancy. Our human nature was superseding the bounds of what we considered the natural world.

Tim was now born into our stream of mutation. We didn't know if KK and I would be his equal someday. His strong will and aura of power made us followers. I was uneasy with the change but I felt safe with Tim. He was a Twelve.

Tim walked ahead with determination and assuredness as if he had known what lay ahead. The quickened pace made KK fall behind. She and I were getting tired. Tim seemed to have boundless energy. He turned towards us with the warning, "We must hurry! Trouble is headed our way." We couldn't doubt his forewarning but wondered when and what we might be facing.

Our feet had become calloused so the rocks and debris on the ground didn't bother us. Tim's fast pace wouldn't have left any time to recoup from pain anyway. Tim took away our worries of planning and caring about our next move.

After hours without conversation and only a couple short breaks, Tim stopped and turned towards us and said, "Let's rest for the night and talk." He pointed at small hill. We found a hole going down ten feet. It made a great den for the three of us. Tim had sensed this location. This was a perfect spot to rest and hide out from the roaming dangers above.

Our stomachs were empty and our tongues were dry.

We couldn't gather enough saliva for a decent swallow. KK opened the bag of supplies and pulled out a bottle of water.

She asked, "Do you want some?"

"Sure."

We took turns sipping from it. We had stretched beyond our limits. Lucky for us, Tim had stayed strong enough to keep the bag as he was escaping from the garden. It felt good to be together in our den feeling the warmth from our closeness. Huddled closely, we fell asleep.

We awoke very early. Tim dug into the supply bag for food. He had packages of beef jerky. He gave each of a package and a bottle of water. I was worried about using up too much of our supplies. Tim seemed to sense my uneasiness and let me know everything would be fine. I then eagerly ate and drank. KK had no second thoughts.

Tim was ready to talk.

"I understand our powers and I share in all of them," he told us. "There is more to come, and we will become key to human race survival." He let us know we'd be changing soon and when we did, our powers would be equal and more powerful than they were today. This message made me curious and anxious. I wanted to know how soon and how different. Tim did not elaborate.

He predicted the aliens would return for revenge. He said, "They'd come in large numbers expecting to annihilate us. They would have weapons beyond any we had ever seen on Earth. The aliens wouldn't expect any resistance except for the existing in-cohesive hostility." He explained they'd be here to destroy and not to inhabit. We were key in fighting the aliens but he didn't know what it meant. He knew these things as we knew things in the present.

We were three kids fighting for our own existence on what was left of our planet. According to him, we were now the human race protectors. I didn't doubt Tim. I doubted our ability to take on the aliens. Fighting the aliens in Home Fort Twelve was almost fatal. Taking on an entire army was beyond my imagination. I didn't have the level of power Tim had. I wondered what we would become to enable us to defeat an army.

We had at least another fourteen days of traveling to Home Fort Fourteen. We climbed out of our hole. Tim marched ahead. There were no large hills, wreckage, or buildings in sight. We saw no signs of life, alien or otherwise which was good because almost all of our encounters with other forms of life since doom-night had been hostile.

We were moving along with a few interruptions of conversation or changes in direction. The path ahead became hilly with crevices and high banks of mud. Our pace slowed down accordingly. The hills became steeper and steeper. It was hard to reach their tops without crawling.

There were remnants of civilization in little stream beds. At first, it was pieces of houses or scraps of garbage. Finally, on the ground, flies were covering a dead dog. The smell of rotting bodies was in the air. We had no interest in the dog except to note it was a sign that life could be nearby. We'd have to be on guard for cannibals and militants while keeping in mind the sick and frightened animals on the prowl for food.

Tim started up a hill ahead of us, when suddenly he slid back. I avoided him by jumping to the side. He came over and hugged us for the first time as a threesome. The energy changed me and overwhelmed me. I felt the warmth of Tim and KK. It was stronger than anytime KK and I had hugged. My mind melted into theirs. We were now one being, sharing our new powers. Tim, KK, and I were no longer entirely individuals. My world had changed again. KK and I both were part of Tim as he was part of us.

Our look-feel showed an open area with buildings and

houses. I remembered seeing the towns between Home Fort Fourteen and us. We still had the map Tim saved, but it wasn't the right time to play detective. I hadn't looked at the map well enough to remember towns.

Tim sensed the people ahead. While hugging, we felt their presence. They could be friends or foe. We could count heads and notice activities. We couldn't register their feelings or attitudes. There were a huge number of people, perhaps in the thousands. That number so close to us, was enough to send Tim reeling.

We felt people spread out over a wide area. We'd had to be especially careful going forward. Tim's reaction was enough to put us on guard. We hardly spoke about our approach. It was simple. KK glanced between Tim and me. We nodded with approval and understanding. Our plan was to have our pistols ready and to stay close together. We knew nearness increased our new powers. With the numbers we had to face, our first plan of action would be to retreat at the first sign of danger.

I took the lead, with KK following right behind. We were armed. Tim carried what was left of our supplies. I couldn't move as fast as Tim could. The ground was more level and so our exposure was greater. We couldn't lie low jumping from one ravine or dip to another to avoid discovery. As we neared the dwellings, the look-feel sensations grew stronger.

I caught sight of an inhabitant. It was a young woman coming over a small hill. She was calm and not frightened of us. I instinctively reached for my pistol grip. KK shared my intensiveness and before seeing the girl, she pulled her pistol out. We stopped and waited for the young woman to reach us.

She called ahead and asked, "How are you doing?"

She was friendly to strangers and not suspicious. Maybe she hadn't come upon desperate attackers.

I yelled back, "We are hungry, thirsty, and tired."

She reached us before answering. She looked well fed.

Tim came forward asking, "Can you help us?"

She said, "Sure." Then without pause, she grabbed Tim's hand and led us away.

We were still apprehensive. We didn't take our hands off the pistols. Our ragged appearance didn't seem to make a difference to her. She put us at ease with her demeanor and lack of fear.

Tim asked, "What's your name?"

"Willa."

"My name is Tim and this is Brock and KK."

The big open pit amazed us when we got to the edge and saw how much was intact. Our visions hadn't prepared us for how normal things looked. Trees were still standing with brown leaves as they are in the late fall. There had been no fire and the mudflow missed the town. We could see the dried cliffs of mud surrounding the town just like our village but they had stopped short of causing a lot of damage. There were no cars or trucks moving around. There were many people standing in the clean streets visiting. We saw no burned or injured people. The residents somehow avoided the hot electrified shock wave from doom-night. The dirty rain we experienced early on had colored the entire place brown. Green lawns were smashed down and covered with brown goop.

Willa pointed towards the center of town and said, "We'll be there in a jiffy and all will be okay." We leapt down the mud cliff. Along the way to the center of town, we passed others. They waved and said hi to us. It was hard to understand the calmness of this place since everywhere else had been devastated.

A police officer stood in a dirty uniform in the center of town, outside the city hall. Willa led us straight to him. He was formal and not as friendly looking as everyone else was. His badge read "Galena PD."

He asked, "What are your names? Where did you come from?"

When the questioning started, Tim looked at KK and

me to deliver a message. We were not to mention the forts. He wasn't sure these people would remain as friendly. Our new skills and rugged appearance made us oddballs to them and we could become alienated either by them or through our own actions.

The officer took notes as we answered questions. He wanted to know what we had experienced before arriving in this town. Tim recounted our narrow escapes from the cannibals while leaving out how we had gained incredible new powers. KK warned him about the rats searching for food. We explained how we gathered food from our town until the militants arrived. I described seeing the spaceship landing and then blowing up as it was under attack. Willa stood by and listened to our tales of woe. We had questions for him, but before we could ask them, he dismissed us.

Willa took us to an old restaurant for food and drink. The restaurant had a red counter with swivel stools. Along the wall, there were booths with torn seat covers. We stood in line to get food. Willa explained that their small river town had become a large central depot for nearby cattle feedlots. The local warehouses were filled with cattle feed, straw, and hay. Their city council took control with the small police force to ration out food. They calculated supplies would last for a year without any more catastrophes. They didn't mind bringing in new people because many elderly had died during doom-night. Newcomers were rare and provided them with important information on how others were surviving.

The city council set up committees for food handling and protection, refugee resettlement, supply replenishment, and security. Committees created policies and new laws. The security committee hadn't done too much because they had no sense of urgency. They had raided the local National Guard Armory to collect and distribute weapons. They instituted mandatory weapons training. Willa said, "They expected us to visit with them because they'd want to know about the different threats and especially anything we knew about the aliens." We couldn't reveal too much about the aliens and their weapons without letting them know about our face-to-face bout.

At an old restaurant, we met more people. They gave us hamburgers and water. They gave us a small stick with a mark on it. It proved we had been fed. It was crude but sticks were easier to come by than paper. We thanked them as we left.

Willa led us to the high school gymnasium. All newcomers started out staying there until the committee gave them assignments and permanent housing. We asked how the committees made assignments.

Willa said, "Everyone has to support the town based upon plans and rules created by various committees and children were not exempt from assignments."

Staying at the gym was the starting point created by the refugee resettlement committee. It would give us time to find our way around and to learn how they worked together to survive. We could end up assigned to security, food handling, or any other support function. The committees did not allow personal preference for an initial assignment. Willa worked for resettlement. She was a greeter. We finally understood why she accepted our presence so calmly. She had brought in many other newcomers without problems.

We weren't sure what all this meant to us. We were intent on finding Home Fort Fourteen. Yet there was no rush to give up on something so close to our prior life. We wanted to stay around long enough to get our assignments and to caution them, as much as we could, about what perils lay ahead.

The militants, cannibals, aliens, or other predators could well be on their way to this town. It was only a matter of time before the evil roamers would come to do them harm. We knew from Tim's premonition that the aliens were returning for revenge. This unsheltered, unrealistic habitat would be a prime target for their army.

That night we had an uneasy sleep. It would take a while to feel safe enough among our benefactors. Willa arrived early and waited outside for us. We had no showers or toilets. She took us to a bathing area on the edge of town where large holes bubbled up clean water. A short distance away, we found logs used for toilets. She stayed with us until we were ready to return to town. Then she left to continue her duties on the ridge looking for more refugees. She suggested we wander around to meet people and to become aware of the work they were doing.

The people we ran into were too busy to visit. So, we followed and watched them. One group had large baskets and bags. They moved up the cliff. We watched as they gathered up the small things that had fallen from the sky shortly after Home Fort Twelve exploded. We had focused on reaching Home Fort Fourteen and hadn't paid attention to them accept for the short tasting session. After they filled the baskets up, they returned to town where they dumped them into large crates.

Stopping a gatherer, KK asked, "Why are you taking them back to town?" He explained how they had fallen from the sky and how some refugees had survived by eating them. Our earlier tasting session made me realize how important they could be. He gathered them for the replenishment committee. They knew these new things were edible, but they were not ready to abandon the beef. The committee had determined they were nutritious and full of protein. They also noticed their ability to self-propagate.

Two days later, the seemingly inept security committee called us in for debriefing. The three of us stood in front of them as they pried information from us. They repeatedly asked if there were more ships or aliens and we kept telling them we did not know. They did not seem worried about the bands of humans out to rob, kill, or eat them. We tried to let them know the aliens were only one enemy they'd have to face. They knew the aliens were the ones responsible for turning Earth into a desolate mud pile so they feared their power more than any Earthly threat. After an hour, they officially welcomed us and let us leave.

We spent the next six days roaming free, eating beef, and befriending the townspeople. Willa was rarely around to visit. On the seventh day, she informed us our assignments were ready. Our days of hapless meandering were over. We hadn't considered our committee assignments. Our biggest wish was to stay together. We understood that couldn't be our choice.

Willa led us to the resettlement office. They assigned KK to security. I went to food handling and protection. Tim asked for an assignment with me but they denied his request. He had to report to the replenishment committee. The housing committee did not assign us permanent housing. We had to remain in the gym. We were to report immediately for work. The entire process took less than ten minutes. We had split up for the first time since Tim joined us. They took our freedom of self-rule away. We had become part of their community.

Leaving each other every day wasn't easily accepted. One alternative would be to ask again if we could work on the same committee. One day after work, we visited the resettlement committee. They listened to our request and pacified us by saying they'd consider it. We were lost in an inconsiderate bureaucracy where filling slots was more important than caring for the workers. Our resentment was building.

Weeks had passed by before KK suggested leaving. She didn't like her assignment because only a few on her committee understood how much danger they were facing. She worried about the lack of preparation, discipline, and seriousness and knew it would put us in jeopardy. No matter how much she pushed for more weapons and training, nothing changed. At most, she wanted to stay for two more days.

That night Tim rolled around uncomfortably. I soon joined in the unrest. KK picked up the same signals. We woke up knowing an alarm would soon sound. Until that night, we had put our powers on hold. They were not gone but had been ignored. We couldn't ignore them this time. Hugging together, we sensed a horde of people marching towards us. They were quiet and orderly. We estimated five hundred were in the group. They had pistols, rifles, and grenades.

CHAPTER THIRTY-ONE

Onard checked in on me every couple of hours. When I was awake, we talked about our next move. I had to convince the Saviors that the planet below needed cleaning before we moved on. It wouldn't be difficult, since they were witnessing the zirn seedling destruction. The consumption of our crop meant we were off schedule with the planned replenishment. The only way to get close to the needs of Hight was to make sure nothing on the planet survived.

Onard helped me build a presentation arguing for immediate action. I felt strong enough to present my plans to the Saviors. They listened with no interruptions. Onard suggested we recruit the disbanded teams that worked the planet-saving projects because they'd be more than eager to get onboard and contribute to the effort. Their purpose would be to invent a weapon or weapons to eradicate the creatures on the troublesome planet. They couldn't harm any zirn seedlings or hamper the future crops. We would reward the teams and permanently enlist them as our support corp.

My warning about the destruction of zirns before they seeded and grew was the winning argument. I estimated the creatures would consume over fifty percent. With the reduction of output, we'd lose over a million Hightians to starvation. Just as important of a loss would be the reduction of habitat. The grubs could destroy thousands of acres with structures, roads, and fire damage. My plans and hopes called for their annihilation within thirty days.

The Saviors eventually approved the requests but didn't return with a quick answer. Instead, they sent me away so they could discuss the situation among themselves and perhaps come up with other ideas. I was learning they didn't always sit on the sidelines and occasionally, they contributed to the methods and results. Two days passed before Onard and I heard from them.

The Saviors called us to join them, as usual, without a hint of courtesy. An administrator on the monitor reviewed our plan. While listening to him, we both received a detail hard copy. The Saviors agreed to our plan in full. They proposed the new recruits precondition future planets so we wouldn't have to struggle with these variables again. They suggested other types of preconditioning after thorough analysis. For instance, the cultivation process should consider the surface features of a planet but also beforehand during an eradication step. They appointed Trush the leader of our recruits. He had been a member of a failed team. They expected Trush to work closely with us.

After catching up in two days with the video and research material Soya and I had gathered, he immediately contacted us for a meeting. We met and discussed alternatives but agreed to shelve them until he assembled his team. He was happy to bring his team together again because they deserved another chance. He impressed Onard and me with his aggressiveness. It was the attitude required for such a momentous project. Trush thanked us for our input and for the opportunity. He mentioned his team had lost their project the same week we submitted the zirn samples to the Saviors.

He said, "The Saviors shut off many others after your presentation and they still support a few more ongoing operations."

Trush left us and returned in two weeks, one week earlier than expected. He returned with his team prepared to get a go ahead on their plans. He had the scenarios mapped out in a simulation with outcomes based upon varying parameters and statistical probability. Right up front, he assured us they wouldn't harm most zirns, no matter what course of action we endorsed.

The first plan of attack was the most technically challenging and the costliest in time and resources. He wanted to starve the planet of oxygen long enough to wipe out the living creatures. Some zirns would be lost but most wouldn't be because they were in hibernation and they could outlast all others. This plan involved stripping the planet of all air. Afterwards, the devices used to do the job would act as filters or dispensers to reestablish a healthy atmosphere. I could tell Onard wasn't impressed with this idea and neither was I.

Trush's next alternative was much more direct and possibly solved two problems. His team wanted to use brute force by using hundreds of thousands of citizens from our over-crowded planet to concentrate on the pockets of survivors, no matter what species. Orbiting ships above the planet would scan for life and direct our avenging army. They would possess our ray technology, plus weapons with a much greater kill ratio.

Taking this approach would relieve friction from of our planet's hot points. Moving large numbers of people wouldn't be much of a problem for our big zirn planting ships. The bigger problem would be caring for our citizens as they moved around the dangerous surface. There would be injuries, hunger, and fatigue. There were few land transport vehicles available. Our small shuttle fleet couldn't operate with the speed and robustness required for such a demanding operation.

Trush listened to our arguments against both choices. We let him know the second plan was favored and more likely to meet our new deadlines. Our deadlines had changed because pulling the teams together to enact their plans within our original thirty-day limit was unachievable. Regretfully, the delay would allow the inhabitants to destroy more habitat and they would be more adapted to their new situation. We sent him away to solve the problem of supporting the citizens and to figure out how to best get them to participate in our crusade.

I didn't let him know the real reason. I, Wollen, preferred the second approach. It was because having an army of destroyers personally wiping out the horrible worthless grubs appealed to my need for revenge. They had killed Soya and now they were reducing our harvest through direct contact. Our citizens would have the same pleasure. Expediency wouldn't provide as much of a reward as primitive reactions. I planned to take part in the operation myself if the Saviors didn't overwhelm me with too many new projects.

Trush was back to us in two days with a plan we could accept. We sent a message to the Saviors telling them our plans had been set. Trush followed up by commandeering ships, weapons, and supplies required for the cleansing.

CHAPTER THIRTY-TWO

There were men, women, and small children coming directly towards the town. They knew where we were and what the town had for them. The night guards sounded the alarms. This wasn't a test. KK was supposed to join her committee and become a leader of a troop recruited from all other committees. In the drills, it always went well, right up to the point of everyone gathering in a formation for deployment.

We stayed with KK regardless of our given assignments. She was more than ready to take on her assignment, especially since we knew about the attack before any others. She assumed we would follow. It made her feel more secure. At least she knew we would be reliable.

As usual, the troops gathered around their leaders in the correct locations. They had often practiced during random rehearsals. One problem was no one ever went further than the assembly. Each leader knew where to go but they never followed through to the specific assignments. The security committee had chosen the locations but no one had any idea what to do when they arrived. After her first mock drill, KK warned them about the lack of follow-through. The committee gave her their patent answer. They'd put it on a future agenda for discussion.

When the leaders understood this wasn't a drill but the real thing, they were having trouble handling the news. Especially when they heard, the attackers were less than an hour away. This was enough to help set off general panic. When we arrived, KK lined up her team, but when they found out about the army marching towards us they deserted to find their loved ones. They were not disciplined enough to keep their assigned post, let alone take up weapons. The security team hadn't trained them well enough. It was a fatal mistake for the townspeople. The plentiful food supply and absence of devastation had lulled them into believing this day would never arrive.

KK had a couple from her team and us, still with her. It made no sense to guard her assigned position with so few people. The other troops had as many members or more than us. The security committee leaders had deserted or were chasing deserters. We had no one left to lead the remnants. I estimated there were 100 people left including the children. The entire plan had fallen apart. Without a leader, the 100 left would be incapable of defending the town.

KK stood away from us and bellowed out commands. She had taken control. The fragmented groups came closer together so they could hear her. She was loud and strong. She yelled, "Tim, Brock, come here with me!" We moved in front of our newly formed troop. KK was sending mind messages to us. She wanted us to help her by splitting the troop into three groups. They were obedient and didn't question our orders. KK took one group to search for weapons. Tim took his group to gather supplies. I took my group off to find a place to fight and prepare for the battle.

KK went to the pre-assigned defense locations where she knew there were rifles, pistols, shotguns, and ammo.

They picked up as much as they could and piled the ammo on anything they could drag without tearing it. They used pieces of canvas tarps as sleds. The children were having a hard time with the heavy guns. Most of them had at least two items.

Tim headed for the restaurant and the supply sheds behind it. He told his people to gather up as many canned goods, dried foods, and meat as they could. They grabbed up cases of water too. He had them load up two trucks. The trucks didn't start up so he had them push them. They moved to the hardware and linen stores. They loaded up anything that would help carry supplies. They were lucky to find dynamite in the hardware store.

With 100 people to fight off the 500 coming our way, I had to find a place large enough and strong enough to hold up against an attack. It had to be a location where there would be an escape route. It also had to be the first line of defense so it would need to be close to where the attackers would descend into town. I described to my people what we had to find. They inundated me with suggestions. None of them seemed good. Then an older woman yelled out, "The sewer works." I didn't give it a second thought. She led the way.

The sewer works building had thick concrete walls. There were few entrances to guard and it would easily hold our 100. We barricaded windows and doors. I sent a few to scout for an escape route. They were gone only ten minutes. They found big sewer pipes leading out. The pipes were dry because of lack of use. I said, "You need to follow pipes out to determine the best." They informed me that some might go for miles underground. I told them, "We need to know which were shortest, so we could set up booby traps and which one to use for our escape." It had to end far past the sewer works. I estimated it would be quite a while before they returned.

KK and Tim knew where we were. I didn't have to send anyone out to find them. They were tracking my activities as I was tracking theirs. Tim with his trucks was the first to show. Our groups joined to unload the supplies and move the trucks out. Tim had them divide the food into backpacks, sheets, and blankets. They delivered dynamite to the team scouting the pipes. Some scouts had returned and identified short pipes where we would set up booby traps. I visited the area to see how well they were doing. I wondered if they'd have enough dynamite to set traps in the front entrance. No one could answer.

KK's group filtered in, carrying what they did not lose on the way. They positioned weapons by doors and windows, with enough people for each. She told them, "Yell for help to let others know you need help." She spread out six teams of three people each to defend different entries. Each team could hear shouts from their specified support area. They had to stay close to the main hall to help protect our escape route until needed elsewhere. If it seemed our position would become over run, she'd send out a command to retreat to the main hall leading to the outgoing pipes.

It was raining. It was the first real change in the weather in days. We didn't have enough time for a trip back to town. Some scouts searching for an escape route hadn't reported. I instructed Tim to take the supplies down the pipe after we chose it. We took less than an hour to prepare. Tim also gathered up the smallest children, so they could escape along with the supplies. Soon the attackers would reach our location, so KK, Tim, and I joined in a hug. We could see the horde minutes away. We needed to find a way to get them to attack us so the deserting townspeople would have time to escape or hide. Our group was following orders without hesitation.

CHAPTER THIRTY-THREE

It was our first day for cleansing. Trush's plans called for a pilot run to the planet with ships orbiting above monitoring progress. We had quickly thrown together the volunteers, ships, and weapons. The Saviors supported us and publicized our project to the world. Trush, Onard, and I would be on the first shuttle. We'd ensure things went well to watch out for our future and to begin our revenge.

Another shuttle would follow when we made sure all was well. Our scanners found an area close to where my shuttle had exploded. I had them focus there because the grubs were close by. I hoped to annihilate those responsible for my injuries. The area showed thousands of grubs. We had successfully imprinted most of their DNA on our previous visit, on comparison, that left no doubt that the majority of grubs were the same as before. We also knew their strengths and considered them inconsequential.

Our plan was to attract them to the shuttles. Then release our 180 volunteers to provide the first trial under fire. The ships above would monitor us through our shoulder-mounted cameras, our shuttle scanners, and their own video devices. We'd send everything to the Saviors.

We had made sure the ground underneath was solid and able to hold the weight of our craft. Our shuttle landed without difficulty. Everyone aboard was anxious to start the process. We waited and waited for them to come running towards us as they did before. None attacked us. We had scans of a few different creatures curiously investigating but no two-legged intelligent creatures. We were puzzled.

This was too much of a departure from the past behavior to permit the other shuttle to land. We would have to stay put for a while and maybe leave the shuttle to determine why things were different. All of our feeds from the scanners showed the grubs close enough to be aware of our landing. They were in two groups. The largest and closest was moving away from us and towards a stationary group. We guessed they were amassing to defend themselves. Onard and I were disappointed. Trush wanted to leave the shuttle right away with his troopers and attack the first group before they joined the larger group. He wasn't in favor of any scouting trips or surveys.

All of Hight was waiting for our next move. The publicity machines on our planet had turned this into one of our most hopeful events since zirn creation. I wanted to proceed with as much caution as possible. We had underestimated the inhabitants the last time we were here. As a result, the guards and Soya had met their demise. Although my outward disdain for their abilities augmented the confidence and aggression Trush was showing, my true feelings included fear. I remembered the grubs we chased in the tunnels under our shuttle. They were not crazily aggressive as the others but I believed them to be the most dangerous. Soya and I had tried to eliminate them but they had puzzling tricks we never understood. I had a feeling they would present a worrisome dimension.

I contacted the Saviors to report the behavior change

and my fear that the inhabitants might plan a mass attack or trap. Asking for directions would pull them in and make them somewhat responsible for the results. Trush didn't think it was a good idea to bring them in while Onard applauded the move. I gave the Saviors three choices. One was to take Trush's lead and rush out with an immediate attack. The second choice was to send small teams out to lure the inhabitants closer to our shuttle so we could get back on plan. Three was to take off and come back later or land in another place.

The Saviors took no time deciding. Without surprise, they ignored my choices. They said we were to wait it out and give the inhabitants time to come to us on their own. They were not worried about their numbers or abilities since we had superior weapons and intelligence. We were to be patient. I was happy they decided. If I had wanted to wait, I would've wondered if they agreed. We were following orders. Everyone knew the Saviors had given us those orders. Onard and Trush were content because we were still on the planet, primed for attack. They didn't like the delay but having to leave and come back could spell the project's demise.

The Saviors gave us the go ahead for this project because of how well we performed with the zirn proliferation. Other than this slight delay on this planet, our other operations were proceeding on. We'd lose more citizens to starvation in the short term but for the long run, the food crisis was over. The Saviors were already moving forward stepping up plans for the development of other planets. Our roles could be unnecessary and my revenge, with the requisite prestige, fame, and fortune Trush sought, would disappear with an administrative override.

We spent hours watching the results with continuous scanning. Once in a while, we'd see movement towards the shuttle but they never made it to us. Trush was becoming impatient. He again offered to take a scouting party to attack the inhabitants and possibly lure them into a trap. He came up with many plans. Onard and I listened to him but we knew we had to wait, per the Savior's decision.

Almost a day passed by before anyone budged. It wasn't much, but it was something. We notified the Saviors right away. We detected hundreds of grubs coming our way. At first, we thought they were coming for us but they had no order. They seemed to be scattered, moving in our general direction. Trush immediately saw this as an opportunity to run our pilot. He asked the Saviors for permission to start. They didn't hold back. They gave him permission to disembark and proceed with the cleansing.

Trush notified our volunteers to prepare for battle. Onard and I joined the volunteers. The weeks of waiting and preparing made us anxious. I, Wollen, was ready to meet them head on. It would be different this time. I wouldn't end up in a burning pit reconciled to die. It would be their turn to feel helpless and the spirit of defeat. Our powers were unbeatable on this primitive world!

CHAPTER THIRTY-FOUR

As the horde approached town, deserting townspeople ran towards our location just ahead of them. They were aware we had set up a stronghold and wanted to join us. Other townspeople left the area by themselves. They were not ready to defend the town. We opened a way for the refugees to enter. KK took control of them. She split them up to support the defensive positions and others she sent to Tim. Tim could use them to move supplies into the escape pipe when the scouts returned.

Trying to lure the attackers to us was no longer a problem. The stream of refugees brought them to us. We were at the point where no more could enter because the attackers were too close. Townspeople ran in front of them and perished. We were now the main point to attack as we had hoped. With KK in command of fighters and Tim preparing for our escape, we would be more than a match for them. The sewer works had enough fortification to keep them at bay. Unfortunately, the refugees' distractions had left us no time to set dynamite traps in front. I stayed with Tim to help him move things along.

The scouts from the pipes returned. Two of them had

found open pipes leading away for miles. They didn't know in what direction. When we escaped, it would be good to know the horde wasn't at the other end. Tim chose the pipe with the least obstructions. He said, "There's opportunity at the other end." It would be difficult to travel two-by-two in the small pipe and obstructions would hold up the entire effort.

Tim designated three people to clear or knock down as much as they could in the designated escape pipes. When they reached the end, they were to stay to protect supplies. The handlers loaded up with supplies and followed the first three. Tim assigned others to set traps in the unused pipes. He instructed them to put traps far into the pipes and to make sure they were not obvious.

Everything was set into motion to support our retreat. Tim and his crew would make sure our way out was well prepared. The booby trapped sewer pipes would cut off and eliminate attackers. The action hadn't started out front but it would not be long before we'd need to defend our temporary fort. I made it to KK's side. She had gathered up everything she could to block off the main hall for our staggered retreat. We checked every position to make sure weapons and backup support were ready.

I asked two people to walk in different directions to make sure we had found all entry points. One returned quickly and reported all was covered. The other came back with a look of fear on her face. She had discovered a small door that appeared to be a closet entrance but turned out to be a passageway to vents. The facility had vents spread out from one end to the other on the roof. We rushed towards the small door.

We had to find out if there were any other doors to the vents. If this was the only door, we had enough people to defend it. If there were many, our well-coordinated plans may not work. After opening the door, the answer wasn't right in front of us. The maze of vent pipes blocked all views. The only way to find out was to walk the perimeter.

KK and I hugged to find the answer. We saw two more doors. We stayed together long enough to get a fix on the attackers.

The human horde was upon us. KK left for the front. She gave four people weapons and sent them to me with dynamite. We had a little time before the intruders would find other ways in. Our vision showed them moving straight towards our strongest position. I heard the guns and explosions. We had to work fast so we could rejoin KK. We booby trapped the vents and doors. We also set charges by the iron structures holding up the vents. If they fell, no one could make it through the mangled vents underneath the fallen roof.

I left the four people to guard the door until someone came for them or until they could no longer defend their position. I felt KK needed me. As I neared the front, the noise from the shooting grew louder and louder. Explosions vibrated the floor. The air took on the smell of gunpowder. The first guarded position had two people on the floor bleeding and another sitting up holding his head. Their backup team had taken over. I moved to the next position where only one person was still active. Another four laid wounded or dead on the floor. Engaged for only ten minutes, our positions weakened.

I heard explosions coming from the vent room. It sounded as if different traps had been set off because we heard one boom after another. I caught up with the next group of defenders. The original team was in place and the backup team was still in wait. I sent a backup to fetch the team at the vent room door. I sent the others to help the lone person at the previous position. I moved on until I found KK.

KK and I immediately hugged and scanned our positions. All were still intact but most had lost people. We could see the human attackers swarming over the entire complex. We sensed a few had breached a short pipe that could lead to our escape pipe. Before we broke up, we felt the presence of more than just the humans. We saw the aliens exterminating the human attackers. We cringed while watching them burn a hole through one of our walls.

KK sent the message out to pull back to the main hall. It was almost time to blow up the defensive positions and to make our way back to the long pipe. After the vent door guards returned, KK gave the okay to destroy the entrance to the main hallway.

CHAPTER THIRTY-FIVE

As we left the shuttle, our troop created two lines. Both lines headed in the same direction but we split up so we could surround the two already joined groups of grubs. We planned on coming at them from all sides. Spotters with cameras were interspersed among us to provide live pictures to Hight. The grubs outnumbered us, but our t-rays and small sonic grenades used to emulsify their internal organs balanced the scale. We needed to be close enough to throw the grenades while staying out of range.

Right after we, the fighters, left the shuttle, the caretakers followed. The Saviors required the caretakers to prepare temporary quarters and provide supplies for the fighters. We needed to keep fighter strength up and tend wounds as much as possible right from the start. The caretakers were not fighters. They came from classes of Hightians with skills in the medical and logistics fields. They'd be no help with any campaign to destroy the grubs. These medical specialists were against the wholesale destruction of other life forms. The Saviors had often questioned their loyalty. Trush had tested them for these tendencies and had filtered the worst out. Some fighters voiced concerns about caretakers being along and so close to the action.

The grubs paid no attention to our landing. They were together, possibly oblivious of our impending attack. As we marched towards them, we drew from our instinctive ancient violent past and grunted a deep low sound. It had been ages since we were in armies fighting among ourselves or against others but time hadn't erased our innate behaviors. Our combined grunts brought us together and encouraged us to carry on while threatening those ahead.

My rage for revenge grew along with the bonding grunts. I saw a red fire in the eyes of those around me. Trush stayed in front. He was the real leader, driving us into a frenzy towards our target. We were moving rapidly. The terrain was rough. Many stumbled and fell. We headed to the cliff surrounding the grubs. It would be easy to shut them off starting from the top and working our way down the high ridge. We would wipe out any living thing in our way with our t-rays.

At first, our feet kicked up clouds of dust while the in step cadence created a rhythmic sound. Our throats choked from the dust and ash. By the time we reached the cliff, a layer of dirt caked our sweaty faces and arms. The discomfort added to our determination.

When the rain began, it washed away the grime and cooled us down but it didn't lessen our aggressiveness. Mass annihilation of the creatures with a weapon from space would not have satisfied our inner beast. The Saviors knew this because they thirsted for the same savage delight.

I followed the others as they jumped and slid down the muddy cliff. They were streams of grubs moving away from us. They were amassing to fight us. I heard explosions coming from their direction. None of our troops were injured. As we neared, I expected them to attack. Something else had their attention. We surrounded the gathering without consequence.

It became clear why after only a few yards nearer. They were engaged in battle against one another. It was an unexpected turn of events. Trush, being in front, figured it out first. Soon afterwards, the grubs discovered our presence. They became more agitated. A few gained entry into the complex. Their native enemies took them out as they tried to enter. The thoroughly panicked ones on the outside had nowhere to go.

We started with the grenades. I threw my first one and watched as the grubs bloated up at the mid-section. They fell limp to the ground. The grenades made a low booming sound while sending sound waves to expand and destroy soft tissue. We stopped throwing grenades because we had overtaken the grubs. We swarmed into the confused maelstrom leaving them with the choice to turn and fight us or somehow gain entry into the complex.

They provided little resistance as we crowded together to finish them. Trush sent our group back to guard against an attack from the rear. I was disappointed because my feverish need to draw blood hadn't been fully satisfied. Trush was the commander. We had to follow his orders.

As we moved back, Onard spotted more grubs in the road. We threw more sonic grenades in their direction. They rolled over like the others.

I didn't know how many of our troops were killed or wounded but not many. The spotters sent pictures to the Saviors to allow us to proceed. I thought of other ways to take revenge. It was difficult since we knew so little about our potential victims and because I was already partially satisfied from the battle.

Trush was barking out orders in every direction. We knew the defenders weren't disabled. Our next task would be to gain entry and finish the job. There were a few more explosions from sonic grenades tossed into the complex vents. One group cut an entrance into an outside wall. Everyone crowded up to them and edged forward as they made space for us.

Onard and I focused on the buildings and structures. We couldn't afford any surprises that would take away from our well executed operation. Our role was important yet diminished. If needed, Trush would contact us.

CHAPTER THIRTY-SIX

KK's crew had set charges at all inside openings and others along the rooms leading to the main hallway. Someone had triggered them. The massive walls of concrete came tumbling down where the attackers had entered. A few made it through but ran into our blazing guns. There were other open chasms but it would take a few minutes before any attackers could regroup. We knew others had made it in. She ordered everyone to report to Tim. She stayed waiting for the enemy to be within the range of manual charges. More ran in as if they were in peril. I stayed with KK and fired freely.

We waited five minutes that seemed to be much longer. KK gave the order to blow the charges. We would have just enough time to make it into the pipe. It was important to get everyone else out before the explosions. We turned and ran towards our escape pipe. Halfway there the explosions began. No one close to the front windows and doors could have survived the heavy crushing roof. The dusty air tasted like dry concrete. Our nostrils filled with the fine white particles.

As KK and I trailed behind the others moving into the escape pipe, someone coming out of another pipe fired on us. KK stumbled and fell to the floor. I made it into the pipe and crouched down low. They were attacking from a short pipe. I reached out for KK's leg and pulled her into the escape pipe. The attackers ran into the open. I killed most of them and the rest retreated. That gave us enough time to run and escape into our pipe. KK set a charge at the pipe entrance to go off within three minutes. That was enough time to reach the first turn in the pipe. It would protect us from the explosion and cutoff any remaining attackers.

Fifty or more of our people had lost their lives during the attack. The rest were scared and in shock from the battle. It would take all the power of The Twelves to get them to move forward. No matter how many hostile beings were on our trail, we would find safety far away from the sewer works. KK moved faster than I moved and was well ahead. We didn't have time to hug and scout Tim's position.

The aliens were better equipped than the human attackers. From our vision, we knew the concrete wouldn't be as much of a challenge for them. The aliens would once more be following one of our human underground mazes to squash us. This time there were many more of them and they were better prepared. The last time our powers saved us through knowledge and trickery. This time we'd need more to survive. As we were turning, the whoosh of air and concrete dust hit our backs. The noisy blast was hot and the concrete dust stung our arms and necks. We stopped, fell to the floor, and hugged. We learned that the beginning of the escape pipe had blown up and the way to Tim was wide open. We had to catch up with him.

Tim was happy to see us. We described how easily the aliens had taken down the wall at the sewer works. We let him know how close it was at the end, when attackers came out of short pipes.

We had no plans after reaching the end of the pipe.

We three hugged to find out where we had ended up and to get a lock on the aliens. The townspeople looked on as we put our arms around each other with closed eyes. They had no clue to what we were doing. If any of them had powers, they didn't know or were just not letting us know.

This was the first time our vision surprised and worried us. Our pipe ended ninety yards away from the alien campsite. We couldn't reenter the pipe and find a different exit because none existed. We had landed in the middle of a hornet's nest and the hornets didn't know we were there. The aliens at the sewer works were milling about. Our three choices were to sneak away from the camp, wait, and fight when they finally found us, or attack the camp with the element of surprise on our side. The last choice was the best but the townspeople would need to be convinced. They were not veteran warriors like KK, Tim, and me.

The rain was making some of our supplies unusable. Tim had his crew put as much as he could back into the pipe. The townspeople were wandering around with no idea of what to do next.

We called everyone to attention. Tim stood up on the pipe and offered them the three choices. Right away, a few spoke up and suggested we sneak away. Others countered with the wait and see approach. Tim argued against them. An older fellow suggested there might be another choice, but offered no alternatives. KK followed Tim on the pipe.

She said, "We have to attack the camp before the aliens from the sewer works arrive." This prompted a lot of muttering and discontent.

Tim jumped up on the pipe. He reminded them, "We successfully fought the human and alien attackers while escaping. The rainstorm will help us get closer to the ship. We must chase these invaders from our planet now!" Finally, they relented and committed to following us.

Tim, KK, and I planned the attack. Our vision showed

us a large group with shelters set up around the spacecraft. As we hugged again, we could tell the rain had driven them back into the ship or into their shelters. We had an idea how many were present but we didn't know how well prepared they'd be.

Tim suggested we try to take as many of them by surprise as possible. He suggested it was easy since the rain would help cover up any noise and somewhat cover our movement. We estimated that we still had seventy-five able townspeople with us. We would each take a group of twenty-five and approach the encampment from different directions. I suggested we use the guns as a last resort to save ammo and to keep the element of surprise in place. Besides, with the guns we'd have the risk of friendly fire doing us harm.

KK didn't agree with the plan. She wanted to take out the shelters and the ship. Her idea would be to disable the ship's weapons and eliminate those onboard. Again, she proved her ability to plan a battle. Tim and I agreed it was a great idea. She suggested a small team should move to the ship to set delayed charges before the townspeople attacked. She volunteered to lead the team to set the charges. Tim and I would lead the charge against the shelters.

CHAPTER THIRTY-SEVEN

The first explosion seemed dull and faraway. We turned around when the building's exterior went shooting into the air. We saw our soldiers, and the grubs blasted into the rainy sky along with the concrete and dirt. I covered my head waiting for the chunks to rain down upon us. Our small defensive group was far enough away to miss the direct force from the explosions. We had no cover, so the falling debris was hitting us hard. It had badly wounded a few in our group, left some in shock, and two dead. Onard and I escaped without injury. Out of our fifteen, seven could still fight.

Trush's group was on top when it started. The grubs had outwitted us again. A spotter was busily capturing the scene for the Saviors. Debris covered the hole in the ground. Some of our troops were moving and groaning but most lay still. After looking after the wounded, we moved closer to the complex. A few survivors were trying to dig themselves out. Trush was gone. He had been in the middle with no chance of survival. Only those on the fringes had any chance to live. They had wiped out our main force.

We all stood in shock. One moment we were the

victors. The next we became the victims. Our momentum was gone and our leader was dead. We could only rescue a few from the carnage in front of us. I was torn between hate, fear, and worry. I was worried the Saviors would call off our attack or maybe abandon us. They'd seen enough to make them reevaluate the situation. Without a leader and with no direction from the Saviors we felt helpless. We didn't know if we should enter the complex or retreat to the shuttle.

Once we had the able-bodied personnel ready to move, including five survivors from Trush's troop, Onard contacted our ship. After informing them of our situation, he requested more caretakers. He wanted to know where the grubs were and if they were on the move. He was concerned about making the next move. The mission was still in full play for him.

The shuttle's crew reported a group of stationary grubs near the camp. They also let us know ten caretakers were on the way to our location. We immediately became alarmed. We had experienced the grub's cunningness. With them being so close to the shuttle, it could be in danger. Since most of our fighters perished in the explosion and the grubs were perilously close to our shuttle, we asked for reinforcements from another ship.

Onard took command. He decided we should backtrack towards the shuttle. It wouldn't be easy because the rain made the cliffs slippery, and the ground was soaked. We knew the caretakers were on the way to us and our wounded would soon be safe with them. As we grabbed at the cliff, the softened surface broke away. We laid flat and used our knees and elbows to push ourselves upward. The sticky mud caused our feet to pull out of our boots. We wanted to run to protect the shuttle, but this place had us in its grip.

I felt as helpless as on my last visit when the grubs had me pinned in the fire pit. I wasn't ready to give up because we still had our shuttle and another was on the way. We had killed hundreds. I didn't know if we still had the Saviors' support. It was a good sign that they hadn't interfered.

We passed the caretakers and assured them the wounded were not far away. The rain kept coming down hard. The streams of mud almost swept us off our feet. We saw zirn seedlings bunched up on the surface as they floated by. It was good to see them because they reminded me of our ultimate cause. I was there for revenge and for zirn protection. Every grub we eliminated would mean more food for Hightians.

We were close to our camp. Our shuttle's crew let us know the grubs had moved almost into the camp. There were only a few caretakers and technicians there. There wouldn't be any armed personnel to drive them away. If given a chance, the caretakers would be curious and might try to feed and heal them. They loved taking up with orphans, no matter what the species.

Onard stopped us and gathered all into a circle. He made sure we were ready to go in killing. He forbade the use sonic grenades because the caretakers and technicians would be too close. Our first priority would be to protect the shuttle. Five of us would stay and guard the shuttle. The other five were to take out grubs wherever they found them. The shuttle's crew would direct them as much as possible. Onard and I had to roam alone and attack grubs.

We could barely see the shuttle through the downpour. The crew on the shuttle warned that grubs were around the shuttle. The shuttle protectors moved faster than before. They had to come face-to-face with the grubs to ensure they could do no damage. We broke apart. The shuttle's crew sent me to the grubs outside a nearby shelter. I rushed over, t-ray in hand ready to blast them into infinity. As I neared the shelters, I saw them crouching low ready to rush the doors. I had to move around so my shot wouldn't hurt our structures or any caretakers. They didn't have a chance. I had the ray on wide spray to take out as many as possible. Quietly, I whisked them into nothing. I felt exhilarated. I was hoping the crew would direct me to another location. Instead, they directed Onard towards the supply shelter. I waited impatiently.

CHAPTER THIRTY-EIGHT

Preparing for the attack, we hugged again. We saw two alien groups. One was moving towards the sewer complex, another towards the ship. We had to get to the camp before they returned. So, KK moved quickly towards the ship with enough explosive power to knock it down. Tim and I took everyone else and split into four groups. We moved as close to the shelters as we could. We waited for KK to get things in place at the ship before we moved in for an attack. The townspeople were in place around the shelters. Our plan was to open fire simultaneously on the unsuspecting inhabitants.

Suddenly, I felt an overwhelming sensation of pain. It came from KK. She was in trouble. I looked towards the ship and saw a flash like the one we saw back in Home Fort Twelve. The aliens had discovered KK and her companions. I sensed KK was still alive. Immediately, I turned around and moved towards the ship. Tim had experienced the same sensation and quickly caught up with me.

As we approached the ship, we spotted the aliens not far off to our left. We saw KK hiding behind the ship. We heard explosions and weapons firing at the shelters.

The townspeople had made their move. The aliens were distracted long enough for Tim and me to reach KK undetected. She had sent her team off to help with our attack on the shelters while she set the last charges. She watched helplessly when the aliens appeared out of nowhere and made short work of her small team.

The aliens would soon be all around the ship to disarm the explosives and to protect it while blocking our escape. I felt the rush of panic take over. KK and Tim weren't sharing my level of anxiety. They were busy coming up with a plan. Tim wanted us to enter the ship. We could close our eyes and slip through the side. Our biggest risk would be the hostile occupants. KK agreed with Tim. The aliens were moving towards the ship.

Before making our move, we heard a large roar from another ship landing. It sucked air away from us. We were finding it difficult to breathe. The ship was pulling the air under it to slow down with a cushion. If the ground had been dry, there would have been a swirl of dust. More aliens made our disappearance imminent. It also meant fresh reinforcements were there to finish us.

We closed our eyes and moved towards the first ship. We found ourselves in a well-lit large dormitory. The aliens had left a rank odor. There were no aliens in the room. We quickly moved along with Tim in the lead.

Originally, we wanted to slip out the opposite side after the aliens reentered. With another ship so near, we had to change our plans. After a few minutes, Tim found a large closet with clean bedding.

Once inside, we hugged closely. We saw the townspeople hurrying back to our sewer pipe. The shelters were burning and showed no life. The aliens were under the ship removing the explosives. Others were moving up a ramp to enter the ship. The other ship was on the ground where aliens stood guard. A small group was moving towards the shelters. Far away at the sewer works, we saw aliens milling around the exploded ruins.

Everything was in its place except us. We were hiding inside the enemy's spacecraft.

Our chests were ready to explode as the aliens moved into the ship. I felt their presence with a small sense of familiarity. The danger added to the pressure we experienced. At least in the sewer works we had room to move and an escape plan. Not one of us had come up with our next move. The only thing we agreed upon was to fight it out if the aliens discovered us. We knew the chances of a victory inside the ship, where we were outnumbered, would almost be impossible. We had to rejoin the townspeople before the aliens attacked because they needed our leadership and direction. Without us, they'd be eradicated. It was our destiny to lead and protect.

We heard muffed sounds through the closet door. KK pulled more covers over us. Aliens were right outside the closet. We heard them talking. Their speech was nothing like any language we had on Earth. They spoke with high-pitched whistles and a low undertone barely audible to us. We couldn't tell if they were excited, scared, or calm. For all we knew, they were making plans to rip open the closet door and strike us down.

We hugged again to find a safe area outside the ship. It wasn't good. The aliens from the other ship had taken positions around this one. We were trapped! This was worse than the attacks by the dogs, rats, militants, or cannibals because no invisible backdoor would allow us to slip away without bumping into aliens.

We hadn't survived the threats of our new world by waiting for things to happen. We would have to be the aggressors. Again, our element of surprise would be a huge advantage and hopefully, we'd create enough chaos to draw the guards into the ship. We needed only a few minutes to pass through the ship walls, leaving the aliens searching for the internal invaders.

The aliens were near the closet door. Our weapons

would be loud inside the ship. I eased open the door. We hadn't discussed our plan of attack. We didn't need to. Our mind links had bonded us into a thoughtless intuitive unit. The other battles had prepared us for this moment. We had powers beyond a normal warrior. Our quick reactions and precision movements were coordinated.

As we peered out the door, the world went into slow motion. The enemy stood in front of us not knowing we were ready to pounce on them. We could see five near the door. They'd be the first to go. Somehow we'd have to eliminate all of them or at least keep them at bay long enough to draw the guards into the ship. They were bigger than human adults were and looked much stronger, so hand-to-hand combat was not a possibility. I saw small weapons strapped to them. It was too good to be true. We couldn't wait for more aliens to board the ship or enter the room.

I felt the power welling up in KK and Tim. It was as if an aura of invincibility was spreading over us. I was hoping the aliens wouldn't feel our emanation of dominance. They'd see and feel it in only a few seconds. Just as soon as they spread out enough for us to take them all out at once, I would give the signal.

CHAPTER THIRTY-NINE

The grubs were on the run. We stopped their attack on the shuttle. With direction from the shuttle three times, I found and killed grubs. They soon realized we were after them and retreated. The camp was in ruin. I was more interested in securing the shuttle than trying to chase them. The other shuttle would need a secure location to land.

At least the Saviors let the other shuttle come to our aid. Either they still were behind us or they considered the other shuttle already dedicated to us. Our performance hadn't been too impressive, especially when compared to the pre-mission hype. No matter, the job wasn't finished.

Trush's death reminded me of how our guards in the beginning had underestimated the danger. Our centuries of peace and dominance had nullified our primeval instincts. We needed to be more patient and not let our zeal for revenge carry us to the same end. I left the camp to meet with the newly arrived troopers. They'd be ready to run off, blindly seek the escaping fighters, and then attack as we had. They could well end up like Trush's group. I would have to encourage them to plan and prepare well. I explained my strategy to them.

Onard joined me before I reached the shuttle. I

advised that we should not underestimate the grubs because the Saviors would let this go just so far. I suggested we needed a plan. He agreed to help sway the new arrivals. We both knew, with the great work behind us and with our family and friends reaping the rewards on Hight, it could all end. The Saviors had proven their ingratitude before.

In our world, general welfare was important but individuals were only important as long as they were providing a service and hadn't failed. The competitive teams that failed to help provide a solution to our famine became our "spoilers." They lived in the slums of Hight. We were close to joining those outcasts. The Saviors would then use us as an example.

As we approached the shuttle, we saw a few new troops disembarking. They were clean and noisy with the same level of rage we had on our landing. Others were searching for grubs and setting up guard stations. There were still signs of grubs around our shuttle. Their caretakers were moving supplies to the shelters. Onard and I contacted and introduced ourselves to their leader.

The leader reported they had found unexploded explosives and how they had killed grubs. I used that information to segue into suggesting a plan. I explained to him that our guards and Trush were inexperienced. Onard explained how cunning and aggressive the grubs had been in our last battle. I mentioned the Saviors, and I suggested the consequences of another defeat. He was ready to listen.

I suggested we keep most of his fighting troops onboard and send out scouts to find the grubs. We needed to know the terrain, number of grubs, and how far away they were. They were too far away for our scanners to pick up their location. After the scouts returned, we could create a plan to overtake them. He immediately got up and ordered a small party out to gather as much information as they could. Onard and I trudged through the rain and mud back to our shuttle.

We had lost many in the explosion and the caretakers were still retrieving casualties. A few soldiers from the battle were trickling into the shuttle. It was virtually empty. First, we went into the galley for food. Onard and I discussed scenarios for our planned attack. He wanted to make sure we had a backup plan along with an escape route in case things didn't go our way. We knew nothing could be firm or detailed until we heard from the scouts.

We hadn't rested since we arrived and the muddy battlefield had worn us out. None of us could just jump into our beds. We entered the dormitory worried about the Saviors, the grubs, and our chances of success. We were discussing what went wrong with Trush's methods. Others wanted us to use weapons that were more powerful and a few were ready to go home. Going home would be worse than being trapped in this dangerous wasteland.

We split up and started for our bunks when from out of nowhere I heard a booming sound. The trooper next to me moved back and fell to the floor. I followed his lead. There was no time to turn around to see where the barrage of shots originated. We still had our t-rays but in the shuttle, they were useless because they would cause too much damage.

I smelled something burning as the shots took out the others. I waited for a chance to escape or strike back. They had us frozen to the floor alive, wounded, or dead. I couldn't raise my head because they'd discover I was alive. The attackers quit at the same time. I noticed a movement on one side. A grub had picked up something on the floor. I heard the groaning from the wounded. The blood ran over the floor as it pumped out.

I sat up and looked around. The closet was wide open. The attackers had been in it but now they were gone. I didn't see them leave through the door. At first, I was worried about what might happen next. Something had attacked us from the inside without warning and they should still be onboard.

The caretakers rushed in. One wrapped Onard's wounds.

I asked, "Will you be okay?"

The caretaker interjected, "He'll be fine."

Onard said, "Wollen, don't worry about me."

The guards from outside our shuttle rushed in right after they heard the first shots. They were roaming around inside the dormitory. The troop leader from the other shuttle came rushing over. I explained how they ambushed us from the closet. I warned that the attackers must still be onboard. He rounded up the guards and methodically searched the shuttle. I was exhausted and in shock from the attack, so I found my bunk and fell asleep. My last worries were about the Saviors and how they'd react to the slaughter of my comrades.

Part V Deception

CHAPTER FORTY

The aliens were close enough for us to smell their strange body odor. As they moved to their beds, I gave the signal. Tim was the first to fire. KK followed. We caught the aliens completely off guard. Not one of them was left standing or moving. As the wounded rose, we shot them. I kept an eye on the door. We left a gory mess of bodies strewn around the room.

Luckily, it was enough time to lure the outside guards into the ship. We stopped firing at the same time. Tim had spotted something of interest close to one of our victims and retrieved it. KK and I didn't move far from the closet, just closer to the ship's wall, closed our eyes, and slipped out. Our unusual departure went undetected.

Our first thoughts were to return to the townspeople. The hot rain was pouring harder than before and the mud sucked our feet into the ground. There were no aliens left around the ship. We had a clear path back to the townspeople. We hadn't gone far when Tim mentioned he had picked up a weapon on the ship.

KK, our technician, wanted to try it out. It was a cylinder with a small rotating dial on the barrel. The dial was the only hard part to comprehend. The handle was soft and squeezable. She pointed it at a small mound ahead. The mound burst into smaller and smaller pieces until it disappeared. Her father would have been proud.

Our plans had changed. The befuddled aliens were in the ship, most likely attempting to organize a search. We couldn't be sure how much damage we could do with their weapon. At the least, we wanted it to work one more time against the aliens. Tim left to rejoin the townspeople and prepare for our escape. KK and I kept the weapon and walked towards the ships.

We wanted to get as close as we could to create as much damage as possible. Through the pouring rain, we saw a small mud hill behind the ships. We marched through the sticky mud and crouched down behind it.

The two sparsely guarded ships looked large and ominous. We hadn't taken the time to appreciate how different they were to any craft we'd ever imagined or seen. The gray colored outside resembled a porous sponge with a feathered tail section. From our vantage point, the surfaces looked to be soft. Rubber-like off-ramps extended to the ground. The ship stood on multiple tripods that looked too thin to support the weight.

I worried they'd have the technology to discover us being so close. That idea alone created a greater sense of urgency. We couldn't be indecisive or take the time to study the situation.

With no discussion, KK grabbed the weapon, pointed at the newly arrived ship, and squeezed the handle. There was a small pause while the ray from the weapon ate away at the ship's hard hull. KK kept the pressure on while moving the weapon steadily and slowly.

In a blink of an eye and a blinding flash, the ship exploded. KK had hit something in the ship that conflicted with the ray. The ship splintered in a smoky roaring blast.

The splattering mud stung my face. Next, small particles of debris blew past us. Finally, the main explosion knocked us out. KK's genius in the art of warfare and weaponry didn't prepare us for the power unleashed by the exploding ship.

Our newly discovered powers along with our wily tricks had allowed us to stay free until that moment. We awoke side-by-side in an alien shelter. We weren't tied down or guarded. I had bandages around the top of my head. KK's arm was in a sling. Someone had bathed us while we were unconscious.

The lack of guards puzzled me. I suspected the aliens were in hiding, waiting to pounce on us as soon as we tried to escape.

I asked KK, "Do you know what is going on?"

"I am as confused as you."

We both knew this wasn't an opportunity to miss. Our bed was close to the shelter wall. All we had to do was slip through it and run away.

As we were rising up to get away, an alien came to our bedside. We lay still ready to strike at it with the first sign of aggression. The alien was holding a bowl of something hot and was making hand signs for me to eat. I waved it away at first but the alien persisted. I had the feeling it wasn't dangerous, so I took the bowl and risked a small sip. The alien gave a bowl to KK and then left as quickly as it had shown up.

The show of care made us curious and grateful but it wasn't enough to change our plans. As soon as the alien was out of sight, we jumped up and slipped through the wall. We ran as fast as possible on the sucking mud towards Tim and the townspeople. The rain had helped cover our escape.

Halfway back, we ran into Tim and the townspeople. He had keyed in on us being unconscious and was on his way to rescue us. He explained how he had felt a sense of relief shortly before running into us but he still had to find us and make sure we were safe. We turned around and headed towards the sewer pipe.

KK described how we blew up the ship and how it exploded. She mentioned our short stay in the alien shelter. They were curious about the friendly aliens. We had no explanation because we were still trying to understand them ourselves. Our look-feel showed that the aliens weren't on our trail so we moved along slowly. Tim directed a few townspeople to stay in the rear to warn us in case the aliens appeared.

CHAPTER FORTY-ONE

It had to be a nightmare. The guards were screaming. Some were frantically searching for the invaders. Others were attempting to hide. It took only a few seconds for me to grasp the situation. The other shuttle had exploded with the majority of reinforcements. The few that had survived the last battle were ready to escape. Our remaining reinforcements were in shock. They didn't expect the shuttle's destruction. They immediately blamed the grubs although their indoctrination had them convinced that the grubs were of low intelligence, primitive, and easily defeated. The hours afterwards passed in a complete state of chaos.

The Saviors couldn't let the destruction of one of our shuttles go unnoticed. They realized that the lack of leadership contributed to our chaotic condition. They immediately took command of our operation. Their first command was for us to go after the grubs. They wanted revenge and dominance. They let us know we'd get no more help. There would be no more weapons or troops. They ordered the wounded and caretakers to stay with the shuttle. Without caretakers' support, we'd have to carry our own supplies.

There were three dead and two wounded in the dormitory. I and one other trooper survived to join the guards from the other shuttle. We had twenty-four able to fight. Onard wasn't well enough to come along. We armed him and a few other wounded soldiers. We expected them to guard the shuttle.

We scanned the surrounding area for grubs. To our surprise, we detected two inside a caretaker's shelter. We had no report of their capture. I left with four troopers to bring them in. It would have been useless to admonish the caretakers for caring for the enemy since they didn't recognize enemies to begin with. Before we reached the shelter, our shuttle informed us that the two grubs were on the run. I decided not to go right after them. None of us had rested from the last operation and the emotionally drained guards from the other shuttle were not ready to chase after dangerous grubs. Every time we had attacked the grubs head on, they came out ahead.

Two of our wounded volunteered to help guard the shuttle with Onard. There weren't any others able enough to help us with finding the grubs. We were desperate, tired, and afraid. After making sure the shuttle guards were in position, I suggested that everyone else rest. Our strength, courage, and desire for revenge would revive after resting.

The rain had stopped. I rounded up the troop while making sure Onard and his helpers were still vigilant. If we lost the other shuttle, the Saviors could abandon us or send in troops to make us pay for failure. This would be our last chance to prove our worth to the Saviors. As we marched away from the shuttle, I understood failing to destroy these grubs would mean our end.

Our shuttle tracked the direction of their escape until they were out of range. At first, we moved along cautiously but the more we walked the more our hatred increased. We talked about how we would leave none alive. We moved along at a quick pace. I saw nothing to stop us. Our senses were on edge ready to warn us of any trap or attack.

Suddenly, as we moved over a small hill we caught sight of movement to our right. We stooped low to the ground. The light was dim. The ground was dark and seemed to be moving. At first, it looked like a dark carpet floating along the ground. I realized it was thousands of small creatures headed our way. Our nostrils filled with the stinking, sweaty smelling breeze coming from their direction.

The small flying creatures had attacked me on my first visit. A different challenge confronted us. They were a horde of furry four-legged creatures. As I looked around in other directions, I realized they were closing in from all sides. Our shuttle was too far away to have warned us.

I yelled, "Keep going forward!" We lined up side-by-side, one facing the front, and the next facing the rear. We put our t-rays on wide spray and walked. It was awkward for those walking backwards on the slippery lumpy ground. We couldn't afford to let the small creatures reach us because at close quarters our t-rays would be too dangerous. After that, we'd only had our arms and legs to fight them.

We were rapidly moving ahead. The small creatures were relentless, quick, and fearless. They emitted small squeaky noises. Their intensive attack was wearing us thin. Someone fell to the ground and others helped him. As they helped him, two others fell. The ravenous creatures were gnawing through their uniforms. We heard the clash of teeth when they attempted to bite through the t-rays and metal fasteners. They attacked anyone that came to aid the fallen.

Panic overtook us. Our line was broken. Three troopers were now trying to swing or knock the creatures off. They panicked and ran forward. Without the t-rays clearing the way, they had no place to step. Each tripped and fell to the ground landing on the creatures. As soon as they hit them, they were covered shoulder-to-shoulder by creatures ripping at their flesh. As one went down, I heard a faint yell, "Wollen, Wollen!" Then we heard muffled screams under the massive number of predators.

I considered firing on the mounds of predators to give the fallen mercy. I didn't because their bodies were a distraction. In fact, taking time out for only a few seconds could lose the battle.

CHAPTER FORTY-TWO

We reached the sewer pipe. The aliens were still not on our trail from the ships. There were fewer townspeople than before. The aliens had killed thirty of them during our attack. Our supplies were still intact. Booby traps were set along the escape pipe in case the aliens followed. That used up the remaining explosives. We assumed it wouldn't be long before the aliens came after us. We had to move along.

Tim stood up on the sewer pipe. He called all to gather round. He announced, "We are going on a long hike." They were confused and asked, "Where are we going?" Tim said, "We are going to Home Fort Fourteen." The townspeople stood with blank expressions on their faces. No one had heard of Home Fort Fourteen.

Tim explained, "One hundred underground forts were created by the government for American VIPs. They built the shelters to care for up to 200 people for two years. We had stayed in Home Fort Twelve before coming to your town. Home Fort Fourteen is the closest fort. You have a choice stay here or come with us."

"Are there questions?"

One person asked, "Why didn't you stay at the other

fort?"

Tim explained, "The aliens landed on our fort and destroyed it along with their craft." He didn't mention the computers, satellites, and entertainment center. I felt a few townspeople already found his story unbelievable. KK spoke up, "We estimate it will take at least twelve days to reach the fort. We must start now." Eight people separated from us and walked out of sight.

We thought if we could reach and enter Home Fort Fourteen before the aliens or another peril overtook us, we might have a chance at survival. Tim had given the townspeople hope. After leaving their once safe town, they hadn't thought about a destination. Most were smiling ear to ear. The semi-reluctant ones eventually joined the atmosphere of happiness. We, The Twelves, had taken our place as leaders and caretakers. We had found our destiny.

KK, our organizer, assigned supplies to individuals. They'd be our porters. I took charge of able-bodied people with weapons to be the security force. Tim sat with older townspeople explaining to them where Home Fort Fourteen was located. They were considering what direction to choose. The trip through the sewer pipes mixed up our sense of direction.

The security force spread out along the line of porters to protect both supplies and porters. Tim would be in the lead making sure we moved quickly in the right direction. KK and I would take up the rear to help stragglers and act as a rear guard. Tim had listened to the older people and assured us he knew the way.

Tim stopped the preparation work and called a recess. We were exhausted and sleepy. He gave us three hours to rest with no shelter and a muddy ground. The break made us realize how cold we were. Some went into the sewer pipe where it was stinky, but dryer and warmer. Others cuddled up on the ground, sharing each other's heat and shielding each other from the wind.

Tim didn't rest. He waited out the three hours before he started yelling,

"Everyone get up. Time to leave." At first, everyone was moving slowly. The recess was a mixed blessing because afterwards we felt the ignored aches and pains. It took fifteen minutes to get the porters loaded and the guards in place. Tim stood on the sewer pipe watching things come together. Before we were ready, he went to the front and marched forward towards Home Fort Fourteen. Everyone else hustled to follow along.

KK and I watched the porters as they passed to make sure they were well loaded. She had taken her arm out of the sling to direct porters. She had created a buddy system for those with heavy loads and for the few old and weak. The buddies would share the loads the best way they could make it happen. Once again, she had proven how good she was at organizing projects. As the last porter reached us, we fell in behind.

It was tough going at first. The young and the old made us stop to rest too many times. We considered leaving them behind and coming back after we found the fort. Since we didn't know how long it would take to find the fort, we abandoned that idea. Others suggested we stay put. The majority didn't like waiting in the open for the horrible terrors to overcome us. We knew there were only two choices and Tim let them know what they were. He told them they could stay here and risk their lives or come with us to a safer place. As he directed everyone to stand up and move, no one lingered. The strong helped the old and weak and the porters switched loads with other porters while non-porters volunteered to share the load.

Hours passed in silence except for noise from our stumbling and marching. Tim joined us and we hugged together to search for the aliens. We didn't feel their presence nearby, so we focused on the ship's location and the alien camp. The impressions were enough to get a rough estimate of how many were in and around the ship and how many were in the shelters. We traced our trail from the camp and detected the massive pack of rats. Not too far from them was a pack of aliens moving quickly away. We estimated there were twenty headed away from us. The rats had them panicked enough to forget about tracking us. We were happy to know they were going in the wrong direction, but realized we couldn't count on them being off track for too long. Eventually they'd get their wits back and be after us again.

CHAPTER FORTY-THREE

The swarm of creatures was winning the battle with numbers and mass. I yelled, "Run, Run." Running over the rough terrain had us stumbling and falling but most kept ahead. The new enemy was literally nipping at our heels. Another soldier went down and the creatures soon smothered her. One soldier exhausted his t-ray on the creatures, yet they were not repulsed. I was running for my life. A wrong change in direction or a pause for retaliation could be fatal.

It took time and distance before we escaped the slower-moving creatures. We were all exhausted and scared but not ready to quit moving. The original mission had been on hold. We had to make a big circle to get back on the original trail and to avoid the four-legged brown ravenous creatures.

The exhaustion took hold. We stopped to rest. We set up camp so we could rest, eat, and sleep. I assigned rotating guards to the perimeters. Everyone rested and ate rations. A few soldiers gathered up the small zirns and cooked them.

The soldiers were holding up well considering knowing that the Saviors were ready to abandon us after the grubs destroyed our shuttle. They had escaped the small brown creatures. They had to be building up reluctance, fear, and resentment. Our expedition to wipe out the inhabitants was turning out to be a suicide mission.

More time had passed before I was ready to move on. I first checked out every soldier to make sure each was ready to go. We reported our lack of progress to Onard. He relayed the information to the Saviors. The Saviors never lost track of us no matter how hostile this planet had become. I took the lead. We had to stick together to the end or we would have no chance to finish our mission. The Saviors would surely abandon us on this hellish planet.

Our circling worked. We found the grubs' trail. I immediately reported to Onard. We had to keep him and the Saviors informed or they could shut us off. The trail was easy to follow. Earlier we passed what seemed to be their camp. There were many foot prints and areas smoothed out for sleeping. Some provisions were still intact with paper wrappers strewn about. They had left in a hurry.

Rain fell shortly after we found the trail. The ground turned into deeper mud and the tracks of our prey were slowly washing away. Without the tracks, our best alternative was to continue going in the same direction. I had one of my strongest soldiers run ahead while their trail was still visible. At least, we'd know if they'd changed directions in the immediate vicinity. He went quite a distance before the trail was completely gone and shortly afterwards he returned with nothing to report.

Our pace slowed down to a crawl. The rain was torrential. We sank deeper and deeper into the mud. We couldn't see what was ahead because of high ridges surrounding us. Water erosion had caused dangerous crevices. With no trail, horrible weather, and mud, we had no choice but to stop and wait out the situation. My soldiers were happy to stop and rest again. We were finished for the day. We set up our shelters in the widest open area we could find. I fell asleep before positioning guards. My fatigue was impairing my performance as a leader. As I slept, dreams of attacking the grubs in the rain pestered me. The warmth and pounding rain on my shelter lulled me into a deep sleep.

I awoke to shouting coming from the other shelters. As I jumped up to look out, grubs rushed in and knocked me to the ground. I heard myself shouting like the others. Their surprise assault enabled them to overpower me at first. I couldn't see how many were on top of me. I kicked and swung my arms. As soon as one fell away, another crowded in and grabbed me. I was lucky enough to make a few direct hits to their heads. Eventually, I had knocked them all out. I searched for my t-ray and sprayed the floor. They were gone.

I set my t-ray on narrow and left the shelter. There were wounded and delirious soldiers walking around in the camp. I entered the shelter next to me and put away four grubs. Leaving there, I saw two more coming out of another shelter. I eradicated them. Turning around I found them running towards me. A couple more on the edge of camp used weapons to shoot projectiles at us. Some had big sticks in their hands and others were lifting their arms to throw rocks. A rock hit me in my shoulder and knocked me over. I raised the t-ray up and swept the ray toward them.

Two soldiers had escaped the initial attack. They were firing at the grubs from a high ridge. They couldn't help the others in the shelters without taking a chance of killing them. I moved to the next shelter; it was empty. I entered the next one. I saw a soldier lying on his cot. A grub in the shelter grabbed my arm and tried to flip me to the ground. It didn't have the weight or strength enough to make it happen. I swung one leg up and felt the blow break his bones. It went limp as it fell to the ground. The soldier was dead with a crushed skull. I was too late for him.

I heard a multitude of grubs yelling battle cries. We had no signal for retreat. I ran one time around the camp yelling for everyone to follow me. Without looking back, I scrambled towards the soldiers on the ridge. They were standing on the ridge shooting over me. As I dove behind the ridge, I heard the thundering footsteps from the fanatical screaming grubs approaching the camp. They had a wind-driven odor preceding them that fouled our senses. I moved closer to the two soldiers. I put my gun on wide and readied myself to fire. Five more soldiers joined us. Two of them didn't have t-rays. Two of our wounded and confused soldiers were in the camp below but no grubs were visible. Then from beyond the camp, we saw flashes from inside the crevices.

As the fanatical grubs entered the camp, we fired. At first, they ran wildly towards us. They soon realized our weapons made the direct attack futile. They became quiet as they ran away and hid in crevices but not before, we killed hundreds of them. Darkness was setting in and I was sure they could be more dangerous in the dark.

Part VI Revenge

CHAPTER FORTY-FOUR

We felt tremors of tension. An unseen force, capturing the waves of emotion sweeping our world, forced us together to tune in and check on the aliens. We saw a mob of thousands of people advancing on them. For now, the aliens were eluding the mob. This roaming mob was as worrisome as the aliens. If we led them to Home Fort Fourteen, they would overwhelm it.

As we huddled tightly together, we heard the call from the others. The faraway others we had been ignoring were clearer than before. They were searching for safety and knew we existed. We didn't know where they were or how many were reaching out to us. We knew they were like us. All were young with the same powers as us, and possibly more. We couldn't spare the energy or time to explore these other minds. Our focus was on eluding or destroying the aliens. We passed a message to them about the dangerous aliens.

We learned how to turn off the channel to the others. It was important to find out about them. We couldn't be too sure of their motives. We didn't want them to know about the fort system. Maybe later, after we felt safer when we didn't have aliens and the mad mob on our trail we could afford to explore. Regardless of our suspicions, knowing they were like us made us feel more comfortable.

We needed to take the offensive against the aliens. Running away from them let them be in charge. Up to this point, our aggression had paid off. KK knew what I wanted. She knew it was up to her to plan our next moves. We agreed not to involve the townspeople. Tim ordered them to move towards Home Fort Fourteen. He let them know we would be guarding the rear.

As soon as the townspeople were out of sight, we moved towards the aliens. We closed our eyes to envision the path back. It was clear and much less dangerous using our look-feel. The aliens were scurrying away from the mob just as they had run away from the rats. The rain had let up, but the ground was still soaked. There were fewer of them and they were staying together. They would be on edge after the mob attack. There would be little opportunity of surprising or catching them off guard. Engaging them straight on would be suicide. We would have to outwit them as we did before.

We, The Twelves, were again alone and preparing for battle. Our look-feel let us know where they were, so they couldn't surprise us. KK wanted to leave a trail where they could track us. Then lead them back into the mob. The trick would be for us to elude the mob.

It took hours to get close enough to them. The mud had slowed them down and it made our travel more difficult. The mob was only thirty minutes away. We were also feeling the presence of aliens very near. KK wanted to turn them away from the townspeople and Home Fort Fourteen. Her real intention was to point them back towards their ship with the mob on their trail. We were searching for the right place to spring the trap.

If everything worked according to plan, the mob would kill all the aliens. If it turned out differently, having the alien survivors close to their ship could as before send them back to space. It would be a tough job staying one jump ahead of them. We were counting on them still wanting to engage us.

Turning them around without having the mob cut us off, made us make a wide looping turn. After a while, we stopped and hugged tightly. This was an important turning point. We had to make sure the aliens and the mob took the bait. They were on our trial but something beyond the mob caught our attention. It was a massive pack of rats. The rats hadn't given up on the aliens. The mob had cut in between them so they became the rats' primary prey.

KK suggested a change in our plans. It counted on precision timing and assumed the aliens would fight off the mob so the rats could attack them. She wanted to lead the aliens in a circle. We'd take them between the mob and the rats. As they fought off the mob, the rats could move in to do more damage to both sides. Passing near enough to the mob while ensuring they noticed the aliens following us, counted on perfect timing. KK sketched out her plan.

We were tired by the time we made it close enough to the divide between them. At least we didn't have the townspeople to worry about or to get in the way. The rats had spread out and lagged behind more than before. The mob was about to catch up to the aliens. Our timing seemed perfect.

Tim, with his enhanced intuition, led the way. When the last trailing human was out of sight and as we made it just past their trail, Tim screamed out. The aliens hadn't seen the mob. They were right behind us. I felt a wave of fear making me numb when I realized how close we were to them. It took all the courage I had to join in with Tim. One false step could mean our well-laid plans would fall apart. The mob could catch us, the aliens could beam us away, or the rats would eat us. As I screamed loudly with fear, Tim and KK raised their voices higher.

Our screams were enough to alert the mob. We

scrambled to make our escape. The mob rushed towards the noises and caught the aliens in our trap. There were shots coming from the mob.

We needed more help. We turned towards the rats and angled towards the edge of the horde. Just as we turned, the shots got too close. Tim jumped down between two small mounds. I fell at the end of his feet and KK followed. Our pursuers couldn't see us but they knew where we were. Staying in the ditch would allow the mob to catch us. If that didn't happen, the rats would pour in on us with their smothering bodies. We caught ourselves in our own trap.

CHAPTER FORTY-FIVE

We heard the fanatical grubs crawling along the ground. There were too many of them for us to stay and fight. We had six t-rays and counting me, eight soldiers. Our mission was to catch up with the grubs that blew up our shuttle and not take on thousands of maniac fighters. We named the grubs the shuttle grubs because they had destroyed our shuttle.

We had to appease the vengeance for the Saviors. We couldn't claim this effort as ample. The Saviors were too wise to fall for a lie. We had to show them we could follow their orders.

While the fanatical grubs were lying low, we moved out in the same direction as before. There were no tracks to follow for the shuttle grubs. Darkness made the gummy surface harder to traverse.

After we were far enough away from the fanatical grubs, we turned our t-rays into lights. The t-ray guns were the only things keeping us alive. They were still warm from the action at the camp. The lights were strong and kept us from falling into a hole or tripping over debris. We heard the fanatical grubs coming up behind us, so we picked up our pace. They would have an easy time of tracking us because our feet sunk down into the ground with every step.

We traveled for hours without a sign of shuttle grubs. The soldiers were ready to stop and rest when we spotted tracks. There were not as many as before but they were our only hope. A couple soldiers doubted these were the grubs that had attacked the shuttle. Another complained because there seemed to be only three individuals. I personally worried about finding the tracks so easily; I'd experienced their trickery on my last visit. The conveniently appearing tracks were curious and suspicious. I couldn't dwell on it too much because I had to convince the soldiers we were making the right choice.

We stopped for a short rest. I used this time to bring up the issue. I asked, "Do any of you have any doubts about our direction?" One replied, "You were too quick to follow the new tracks." I put the burden back on her by asking for an alternative idea. She had no answer. I suggested we turn back to fight the fanatical grubs and ignore the tracks. That did not appeal to them. I agreed with them. We were taking a big chance. I argued it might not be our only chance. I suggested following through with this choice, then afterwards, we would have time to follow up on other alternatives. It wasn't a strong argument. It was enough to get us moving again especially after the wind blew the taint of grub odor into our nostrils.

We knew from fresh tracks that the shuttle grubs couldn't be too far ahead of us. I imagined their surprise as we moved closer and closer. My mind was playing tricks on me. I thought I saw them struggling to get unstuck from the muck. It wasn't true. They were barely keeping ahead of us. Once in a while, the wind would blow back on us bringing in their scent, each time it reinvigorated us.

Many hours passed before we saw them. To our delight, they were leading us back towards our base. I shook my head to make sure I wasn't hallucinating again.

As our lights shined over the next hill, we saw the tops of their heads. As we got closer, we saw them waving their arms and yelling loudly. Darkness was lifting. We set our guns on wide spray. Resetting them caused them to beep. A beep meant the power was low. It was another problem caused by our inadequate experience. We never considered the need to pack extra power units. If they gave us one more shot, we would be lucky.

I remembered Trush and Soya. I grieved for the dead soldiers. This planet was my curse. It was taking everything away from me. I might have made a mistake returning. I hadn't gotten close to having my revenge. The planet and the grubs were winning the revenge war. Being close to our shuttle, I considered returning to it and take my medicine from the Saviors.

The shuttle grubs in front ran away. On the left, a screaming mass of fanatical grubs came after us. We had only six t-ray shots between us.

I yelled out, "Everyone wait! Take turns shooting." I passed the word along, "Run after you shoot! Run towards the shuttle!" The two soldiers without weapons left immediately. I planned to be the last one to shoot.

The first shot wiped out the first wave of attackers but others kept coming. The second shot didn't slow them down at all. They were not caring about those in front. After third and fourth shots took out more, the spent shooters were on their way to the shuttle. The fifth soldier did well with her shot but this time she didn't get away. One of their weapons hit her where she stood. I couldn't help her without endangering myself. It was my turn to shoot. I lifted my head to take aim and found them retreating. Instead of shooting, I jumped up, grabbed the wounded soldier, and started towards the shuttle.

I knew the grubs would be after us. My hope was to get to the shuttle, bring in the caretakers, and get permission from the Saviors to depart for home. We had no way to let Onard know we were on the way. If he was monitoring the sensors, he could detect us as we neared. At the very least, the first two soldiers had gotten there well ahead of us and put things into action. I used my last shot to wipe out the lead pack in the swarm of four legged creatures. We had reached the shuttle. Dawn was breaking and the gray gloom returned.

CHAPTER FORTY-SIX

We hugged together to see what the aliens were doing. As the aliens attempted to escape the on-rushing mob, the horde of rats moved in on them and the mob. They went into a feeding frenzy as the smell of blood filled the air. We had made it to the hordes far edge. Our plan to have the aliens wedged between the rats and the mob had worked perfectly.

Tim jumped out and ran. KK followed with me right on her heels. The rats noticed; a small band split off to chase us. We were luckier than the aliens or the mob because we could see where to run to avoid running into more of them. It didn't take long to throw them off or at least distance ourselves enough to forget about them.

As we sat and caught our breath, we huddled together. There were only two aliens still moving. The rats were moving in on them. An alien pointed a weapon at the oncoming swarming mass. As the rats vanished, they left a clear path for escape. An alien grabbed his wounded companion and ran towards his ship.

There were still aliens to chase away. We headed towards the ship. KK was dreaming up another attack. We reached the perch we used to blow up the other ship.

We watched as the aliens argued with each other. The ones in the shelters didn't want to board the ship. They carried the wounded to the ship then returned to the shelters. They were waving the soldiers away.

We, The Twelves had no weapons except our cunning. KK knew the only way to do real damage was to get into the ship again. Her plan was dangerous, but we believed in her. It would mean surrendering to the aliens to gain entry to their ship. There were many risky assumptions. The biggest one assumed the aliens wouldn't kill us on sight. KK's plan meant to put them off guard.

We moved towards the shelters. There were no guards surrounding it. Occasionally, an alien would leave a shelter and enter another. We fell to the ground just outside. Not long afterwards, an alien found us. Staying perfectly still, we kept our eyes shut. The alien left and returned with others. They carefully picked us up and took us to cots inside the shelter. We heard other aliens sounding off as we passed by their cots. They were the wounded. While being covered up, I spotted a wounded alien getting up and walking towards the exit. Luckily, it didn't come over to squeeze the life out of us.

We were there only a few minutes when another group of aliens, led by the wounded alien, came rushing in. They were talking loudly as if they were mad. We stayed still as if unconscious. One of them picked me up roughly and slung me over his shoulder. He wasn't being as caring as the ones that had carried us to the cots. I heard the grunting as the aliens hoisted KK and Tim on their shoulders. I hoped we were on our way to the ship. KK's plan was working. They didn't see us as an immediate threat so they didn't kill us.

Their hairy outcrops seemed needle-like. It was hard trying to stay still. They were powerful and smelled like rotten eggs. My chest registered the heat from the closeness. I heard KK groan. After each step, I felt his shoulder digging into my stomach. I wondered if they might take us to a torture chamber or to a lab for dissection. I opened my eyes to see where they were taking us. They were taking us to the ship.

They marched into the ship and dropped us hard onto the floor as if we were heavy lifeless sacks of potatoes. My head hit the wall. I was stunned. They kicked at us trying to get us close together. They considered us unworthy of respect and for sure, they had never heard of humane treatment. I felt the air rush out as one kick thrust into my stomach.

After a while, I heard the door close. The heat of their presence was gone. Tim was bleeding from the nose. KK was holding her arm. Tim looked at me and yelled "Brock, your head." My head was bleeding from hitting the wall. The blood was running down my neck. KK tore material from her blouse to cover the wound.

It could have been worse. They did not kill us. All three of us still had our mobility except I was feeling faint from the bleeding. We were in a locked room. They didn't know the lock wouldn't hold us in. Above us was a camera, surely with a guard watching our every move. I raised Tim high enough to reach the lens. He took the blood from my head and smeared it over the lens. We were in the lair of aliens. We couldn't wait too long to make a move.

The door swung open. I felt the heat from the alien. It was a heat I'd felt before. The alien stood and stared at us. I doubted he recognized us. We recognized him. He had been in Home Fort Twelve. He had been one of Maria's killers. We stared back feeling the pain from Maria's loss.

The alien was gone. KK stood up, still holding her arm. She pointed towards one wall, closed her eyes, and passed through it. We stood up and followed her.

CHAPTER FORTY-SEVEN

The caretakers did not want to return to the shuttle. They wanted to stay on the planet and help heal it. I presented the problem to the Saviors. They said we could leave them. They were not happy hearing we had barely escaped the ruthless grubs. We were to return home as soon as we could, regardless of probable retribution. The soldiers were ready to leave immediately.

We were preparing the shuttle to take off when a wounded soldier came to the shuttle yelling, "Wollen, Wollen, three grubs are in the shelters." I sent soldiers to find them. I ordered, "Bring them back alive." They would be an unexpected prize. Before the soldiers returned with the grubs, I contacted the Saviors. I let them know we had captured three intelligent creatures. I told them as soon as we got them to the shuttle they'd be able to see them. We hoped capturing grubs would be enough for the Saviors and us to save face.

I had a room set up to hold the grubs. After we put them in the room, the Saviors could watch them. I was hoping they would take more control of our next moves especially on what to do with the grubs. With them involved again, they'd report our mission as a huge achievement and we could return as heroes.

I visited the room as soon as they arrived. They were odd looking and seemed to be staring defiantly at me. I had no interest in finding out more about them.

As soon as I left the grubs, I contacted the Saviors. They were upset because the cameras were not working in the grubs' room. I promised them we'd get it fixed as soon as possible. They'd already announced the capture and were planning to show the grubs to everyone. They told us not to harm them.

Their plan was to get as much positive publicity as possible from our failed mission. The caretakers turned into a planned outpost created to study the planet and nurture the zirns for the benefit of Hight. The Saviors would eventually frame the entire mission as a successful effort. As usual, the Saviors had turned things around for us. They couldn't have their past decisions deemed bad.

I called a meeting for all aboard. I described the sessions with the Saviors. They were worried about what the angry families of our casualties would do. I let them know the Saviors would not let them cause problems.

After the meeting, I sent two soldiers to fix the cameras. They returned in a panic, shouting, "They're gone, they're gone!" I didn't believe them, couldn't believe them. I rushed to the room then sounded the alarm. The cameras stayed inoperable. The Saviors could wait for their show. They would have to wait.

CHAPTER FORTY-EIGHT

We had escaped into a room filled with machinery. It was noisy and hot. We wanted to destroy the ship, but we had another cause. We had to find Maria's killer. He was back on our planet and within reach. KK's plan was to stay undetected long enough to capture one of their weapons and to make sure the killer couldn't return.

Finding the alien wouldn't be hard. We could feel our way to him. Finding a weapon while avoiding recapture could be a dangerous treasure hunt. Our only chance would be to catch one of them alone so we could overwhelm him or at least take his weapon away.

Hugging close together, we waited to feel the presence of an alien. Coming together always made the feeling stronger so we could detect them farther away. As we hugged, we again heard the call from others, the others far away. We joined in thought, feeling the pressure from the interruption. They called us to join them, to give them safety, and to help them control the destiny of our planet. Our joining had enabled them to join our thoughts.

We let them know our situation on the ship and our mission to kill Maria's murderer. They warned us to be careful when using our power to pass through solid objects. Others had perished because they passed into environments where they couldn't exist. They warned us about using our powers to be cruel. They surprised us with the last caution. Thanking them, we took the warnings in stride while letting them know we did not have the precious seconds to help them, worry about them, or communicate with them. They went silent. I wondered who the others were.

We felt the nearness of an alien. Tim pulled tools off wall hooks and hid behind a wide beam. I hid behind a machine that resembled a big air conditioner. KK climbed a ladder and was perched above the door. The alien walked through the door. KK jumped from the ladder onto its back. The alien hit the floor with a groan. Tim rushed to knock him out. I threw my body over his legs. I couldn't hold his legs still. He kicked me off. Luckily, Tim's pounding was taking its toll. The alien lost consciousness.

KK grabbed his weapon and moved towards the door. She yelled "Brock, follow me." Then she ordered Tim to take the weapon outside to our lookout perch. Tim paused for a moment. We knew he didn't want to leave us because he wanted revenge more than us. We were a team, so for him not to follow orders could put us in danger. Tim had to know protecting the weapon was more important than his personal grudge. He left without a word.

We would fight the killer aliens with whatever we could find. I grabbed the tool from Tim. Tim moved back into our former cell with the weapon. They wouldn't look for him in there and he could slip out through the door. KK moved into the hall where she waved me to follow. I knew which direction to take. We couldn't carelessly pass through the walls as we did at Home Fort Twelve. We could find ourselves in a chamber of poison gas. Our best bet would be to move through doors if near.

We kept low and shuffled from one doorway to

another. A couple times, we felt the presence of an alien moving towards us so we closed our eyes and slipped through a wall. KK found a heavy spear-like metal rod. I traded Tim's tool for the spear.

We were near our potential victim but he wasn't alone. In the first empty room, we laid in wait, ready to take on any alien. They'd be more frantic this time because they knew we had mysteriously disappeared the last time we were onboard. Several aliens passed our hiding place. Finally, we felt the killer alien pass our room. He was alone.

KK and I rushed through into the hallway. We were a few steps behind him. We couldn't attack him in the open hallway. As we approached, the others interrupted our thoughts. They were asking us to stop and not take revenge. Tim answered their call by letting them know it was the most important thing we had to do. For me, there was a slight urge to be merciful. I knew Tim and KK would feel my urge. We definitely had to work this out together.

The alien entered a smelly restroom. We followed. He turned away from the door. I raised my spear with both hands high over my head. As I swung the point down as hard as I could towards his lower back, he moved. The spear stuck into his thigh.

He turned around to face us. His arms were swinging wildly trying to grab something for support. KK swung upwards with the tool and hit him in the face. Warm syrupy-brown blood splashed out onto the floor. A strange odor filled the air. He was screaming loudly from the pain. Outside the ship, Tim was sharing the excitement.

The alien slipped down to his knees where KK struck him again. I moved in and pushed him back towards the wall. His blood made the floor slippery. His color changed. KK was still swinging the tool at his head. I felt his warmth slip away as the coldness of near death took over. He slumped to the floor in a bloody mess.

As KK kneeled to strike the final blow, Tim called out to stop. Tim and the others joined us. We melted into our oneness feeling the wisdom and love from them. It was overpowering and enough to stop us from following through with our revenge. This intrusion made me really want to know the others.

The alien's screams had attracted others to the restroom. We moved back to the room we had just left as the aliens streamed toward us and blocked the hallway. We had to risk passing blindly through walls. I closed my eyes and pictured the path used by the aliens to take us into the ship. I detected Tim's escape route. It was the first time I shared the past trails of another.

We had to return the cell. Since the rooms we used to get to the alien were safe, we moved through them and the rooms in between. Everything was fine until the machinery room where we felt aliens in it. More aliens than we could fight.

Our travel through the rooms put us far away from the bloody restroom. KK slipped into the hallway and found a locked door at the end. She called for me to follow. The aliens had locked all doors, expecting them to confine us. The locked doors would hamper the aliens because they couldn't move as freely as we could through them. We slipped past the machinery room. We moved through the locked cell door.

Tim had escaped through the floor. He had gone through two lower levels to the ground. It was easy for us to follow his path. After we hit the ground, it was a short distance to join him. He was on the hill tracking our progress and ready to strike down any pursuing aliens. The muddy ground stopped us from running as we struggled to rejoin Tim. When we came together, we looked each other in the eyes as joy took over our hearts but we fought the urge to celebrate. There was more to do.

As KK took the alien's weapon away from Tim, we heard a roar from the spaceship and felt the blast of hot air knocking us off our feet. The ship was hovering near the ground. KK steadied herself and took one shot at the ship before it blasted off. Her shot hit the ship and caused a small piece to fly off but didn't slow it down.

After a few moments of silence, we realized the aliens had escaped. We had chased them away from our planet, but others were still in shelters. They posed no threat. We had won the battle.

We fell back to the ground, rested, and stared into space. Our thoughts joined with each other and to all others. We described the aliens in residence, the mercy we had given the alien, and how the aggressors had fled our planet.

After resting, KK mentioned the townspeople. I hoped we could catch up with them and find Home Fort Fourteen. We would live a blissful life in Home Fort Fourteen, but the warrior aliens had changed our mission. We would have to prepare to defend ourselves against them. Townspeople would have to help put Earth back together. At that moment, we were weary and dirty but victorious. The Twelves had changed from three kids thinking of themselves to assuming the role of Earth's caretakers. We were strong, willing, and growing.

The others had joined us, yet they were truly a mystery.

THE TWELVES LIVE ON

The sequel Doom Night, The World Beyond will describe life after the apocalypse. The Twelves will need all their courage and newly acquired skills to head off complete annihilation of the human race. As they discover the nature of their unknown helpers they begin to grasp secrets of existence. They find answers to universal mysteries leading them to an unimaginable conclusion.